# YOU PUT A
## *Move* ON MY
### *Heart*
# 3

D1519916

A NOVEL BY

# DIAMOND JOHNSON

# ACKNOWLEDGMENTS

First off, I would like to thank God for even giving me the ability to have the talent of writing. I believe in Philippians 4:13, "I can do all things through Christ Jesus who strengthens me.". This journey of writing has been a tough one, having to deal with school and work but it was all worth it in the end.

To my amazing parents, thank you for believing in me as well, and for not doubting me when I came to you guys with the idea of writing my very own book. I love you guys so much.

Also, to my readers, I would like to say thank you from the bottom of my heart. You guys constantly keep me motivated with the positive feedback. I appreciate the love that you all offer in the book reviews and even on Facebook. Without you guys, this journey wouldn't even be possible, so I thank you.

Lastly, to Mr. Leo Sullivan himself, I thank you for believing in me and pushing me so that I could know my worth. In the beginning, I was writing just to have nothing to be, but you made me take it seriously, and I appreciate all the words of encouragement that you have given me these past few months.

*Diamond Johnson*

# CHAPTER 1

## Malaya Brown

Things had reached the point where my mother and I were barely communicating. Well, we never had a constant communication because she was never really home. But when she did come home, she and I would chill together, watching movies and shit. Now, my mother won't even say two words to me. For some reason, she has this feeling that I'm responsible for the death of my sister and my nephew. Don't get me wrong, it's the truth, but out of all the people in the fuckin' world, how would she right off the bat just assume that it was me? That just goes to show that even after I spent time away in the mental institution and then came back to live with her, she never fully trusted me again. She clearly thought that I was still crazy after all these years. That feeling alone made me want to do some murderous things, especially to her.

It's been two months since Mya and Justin died, and in those two months, my mom had just moped around the house. The only time that she would come out of her room is when she finally got the appetite to eat something. Plenty of nights, I would silently creep into her room and stand over her body as she slept, contemplating the thought of killing her. I thought that if I raised the knife and stabbed her to death, I would be doing her a favor; I would be putting her out of her misery because miserable is what she had been for the past two months. She had lost a substantial amount of weight, she had bags under her eyes, and her hair was even shedding.

If you ask me, her ass was doing the fuckin' most right now. The time that she had to spend with Mya and Justin while they were here, she barely took advantage of it because her ass was always somewhere ducked off with her fuckin' boyfriend. I swear, people like her killed me. The only time she would see them is when they came over to the house. She never took it upon herself to go and visit them in the projects where Mya was staying. But now, all of a sudden, she's in this bitch crying her heart out every night behind their death. Bitch please!

Right now, I was in my room over at my mother's place, standing at the mirror fixing up my hair. This may have been one of the reasons why Jarvis didn't want to fuck with me anymore. I think he was tired of the same old looked that I was sporting. Each time I saw him, I've always had this Chinese bang hairstyle. Shonte switched up hairstyles frequently. Even though she may have had only two encounters with me, I've seen her ass on a daily. I wasn't trying to be exactly like her, but I was just going to piggy back on some of the things that she did.

For starters, I had just finished dying my hair the same burgundy color that was in hers. Mine didn't pop as much as hers did because her skin was fairly lighter than mine, but it didn't look bad on me either. I distinctively remember one time being camped out at her work place and she had her hair in this bad ass bob, so I was trying my best to style it in that same way right now. Call me crazy, but I was going to get that man, even if I had to look similar to his bitch to do so.

As I was finishing up the final braid, my door swung open. I was shocked to see my mother standing there. I was grown, so whenever she came into my room, she usually knocked and waited for me to tell her that it was okay for her to come inside. I don't know what she was doing, but she was starting to look like her old self again; she just needed to gain a few more pounds. I could tell that she must have gone to get her hair done this morning because her hair looked fuller. I assumed that she must have had her hair stylist sew in a couple of tracks for her. Her eyes still had bags under them, but her face wasn't as sunk in as before.

"Umm, Malaya. There's no other way for me to say this. I've been back and forth with thinking about this for weeks now, and I've finally come to a conclusion. You have to leave my home. There's no way that I can continue to sleep in the next room, when I am convinced that you are the one who killed Mya and Justin. I shouldn't have to sleep with one eye open every night because I can't trust that my own damn daughter will not just snap and kill my ass," my mother said to me as her voice shook.

Number one, she clearly couldn't have been sleeping with one eye open every night, because if she were, she would have seen me the few times that stood over her body with a butcher knife.

"I have to leave your home? You saying that shit to me like I'm somebody off of the fuckin' street, Ma! This is my home too! I was raised here! How the hell you just going to kick me out because of some bullshit feelings that you're having right now? If you kick me out, where the hell am I supposed to go?" I asked her.

I couldn't believe that she was doing this right now. Number one, I had no education, so most jobs wouldn't hire my ass. On top of that, I had a fuckin' record, so it made getting a job twice as hard. With no education and a criminal record, how did she expect me to bring home some type of income to provide for myself?

"It isn't some bullshit feelings, Malaya, and you know that! Don't you dare try to downplay the way that I'm feeling right now to make yourself feel better for what you did! I may not have any proof right now, but I know that it was you. When the firefighters arrived on the scene and put the fire out, the police saw that the sliding door was open, which could have been the killer's escape. An escape from four floors high! Two months ago when this happened, your leg was sprained and you had bruises. I asked you where they came from, yet you gave me no fuckin' answer. You did this shit, Malaya! You killed them!" she said, reaching behind her back for something.

As she reached, so did I. I quickly pulled open the drawer in front of me and slammed the knife right into her chest. Her body hit the floor quickly and the gun that she held in her hand fell to the floor. This is what it had come to. She just couldn't keep her fuckin' mouth shut, so I had to do it. My mother lay before me with blood seeping out of her chest. She was trying her best to say something to me, but the amount of pain that she was in just wouldn't let her.

"I killed them, Ma! Damn, are you fuckin' happy now? Is that what the fuck you wanted me to say? I killed that bitch because her ass

4

had a baby by the man that I want, which gave her one up over me, so I had to do what I had to do! Kiss them when you get to heaven for me!" I said, raising the knife and stabbing her a good ten times before her body stopped moving.

With bloody fingers, I raised my hands and closed her eyes, followed by a kiss on the forehead. I swear, this shit felt like déjà vu because this is the same room where I had committed my very first murder. I went into the hallway closet and grabbed a whole bunch of sheets. Once I brought them into the room, I began to wrap my mother's lifeless body inside them. I had plans to clean up all of the blood once I got back.

Dragging the sheet with her body outside, I went to the back door that led to the garage. Once I had the keys to her car in my hand, I popped the trunk to her car and then I continued to drag her body. Finally, I lifted her up and threw her in. After slamming the trunk, I made sure to lock up the house, then I was on my way to drop her body off in the Suwannee River.

In my mind, me killing her was self-defense because clearly the bitch had a gun behind her back, and was about to light my ass up. I guess she wasn't bullshitting when she told me that if she found out that I was the one who had killed Mya and Justin that she would kill me. Hmm, well at least she tried.

# CHAPTER 2

## Jarvis Banks

"This place has been open for months now and I can't believe that this is my first time coming here," Shonte said to me as she walked into my office and took a seat in the guest chair in front of my desk.

I had just finished giving her a full tour of the center, and she was in complete awe at the way I had things running over here. I'm not going to lie, I felt like shit right now for not inviting her to the grand opening that I had a few months ago. She would have loved to come out and support me. It's just that at the time, Shonte had my head so fucked up that I couldn't even fuck with her like that, which is why I didn't invite her. Lord knows that if I could turn back the hands of time, I would have had her there, even if we were beefing.

"You got that *thang* on you, right?" I asked, deciding to change the subject because I already knew where this conversation was about to head, and I wasn't in the mood to be arguing with Shonte right now.

"Yeah, it's in my purse," Shonte said, referring to the gun that we had picked up for her about two weeks ago.

There was once a time when I wouldn't want my girl somewhere carrying a gun, but this is what the fuck it had come down to. I knew I couldn't be up under Shonte 24/7 to watch her every move, so I had to have her carry some type of protection. Truth is, I wouldn't rest until I caught up with Malaya. Out of all the bitches in the world, why in the fuck did I have to get caught up with a crazy bitch who had to do some damn time in the mental institution? On top of that, why did it have to be the sister to the bitch who had sent my ass to prison?

Make no mistake about it, Malaya didn't pump any fear in my heart, but I knew what she was capable of. This was the same bitch who put a dog on my girl, and made her lose our baby. That act alone already had a bullet waiting with her name on it. For some reason, Shonte had this crazy idea that she wanted to be on some Bonnie and Clyde type of shit and put Malaya down together, but straight up, I wasn't that type of nigga. I would never bust my guns with Shonte on the side of me. Certain shit I just wanted to shield her from.

I bought a gun for her protection, not to go around killing muthafuckas because they accidentally stepped on her damn shoe. But then again, I knew why Shonte wanted her part in this because at the end of the day, she was the one who was bit by the dog. She was the one who fell down those flights of stairs and lost our baby, so I wouldn't completely leave her out of the loop.

"You still in contact with your friend that used to know how to hack computers and stuff?" Shonte asked me, looking up from her phone.

"Yeah, why?"

"Because, wasn't somebody calling your phone from private for days at a time? Why won't you have him look into it to see who it was, even though I guarantee you it's that bitch. We just need to know her location. Fuck you be doing to these bitches, Jarvis? You fucked her?" Shonte asked me, standing up from her chair.

I'm surprised that question hadn't come sooner. Shonte knew everything when it came to my hoes. Well, technically I didn't have any hoes anymore because I dropped them all to be with her. I knew I loved the fuck out of this woman when she stood over me a few weeks ago and made me delete every female number out of my phone, besides her and relatives. A nigga didn't have any hoes, and honestly, I was okay with that.

"No, I didn't fuck that girl. I'm surprised you didn't ask me this question already," I told her.

She folded her arms across her chest and stared at me hard. "You expect me to believe that you used to text this bitch all damn day, smiling and shit, but you never fucked her?" Shonte asked me.

"That's what I said, right? If you must know, yes, she did suck my dick, but that was it!" Damn, a nigga wasn't in the mood to have this conversation right now.

"That's when you want to fuck, though! How many times have I got on my knees and gave you head, and in return, you would fuck me to sleep? Please say something, Jarvis, that will make me believe you right now because what you saying to me isn't adding up! I know you, so don't get mad at me for having doubts!" Shonte said. Now she was standing in front of me.

"You want the truth?" I asked her. She nodded her head yes. "She sucked my dick in the restaurant, and I ain't have time to even take the bitch to the bathroom for me to fuck because you called," I told her straight up.

Since I've been home from prison, I hadn't lied to Shonte, and I damn sure wasn't about to start lying to her now. Just like how I knew she would, she tried to walk away, but I had a firm grip on her ass, not letting her go anywhere.

"See how you do? You be questioning a nigga to tell you shit, and the moment you hear some shit that you don't want to hear, you go and catch a fuckin' attitude!" I told her.

She sucked her teeth and then rolled her eyes hard as hell at me. "I don't have an attitude, Jarvis! But answer me this. Would you be okay if I stood here and told you that a nigga I was talking to didn't get the chance to fuck me because you called me? Oh, but by the way, he did eat my pussy though! You got bitches out here sampling shit that you telling me on a daily basis belongs to me, but I can't tell because the first break up we have, you give it away so easily! I hate that I sound so insecure right now, Jarvis, but honestly, can you blame me? You and I done been down this road before."

"No, I wouldn't be okay with that, but I've had worse happen to me! I came home, and the only woman that I ever loved was engaged to some bitch ass nigga!" I gritted at her.

Again, she tried to walk away, but I wouldn't let her. Truth be told, Shonte and I needed this little one on one that we were having right now because clearly she and I were holding on to some things that needed to be aired out. Shonte is the woman who I planned to spend the rest of my life with, so I cared about that way that she felt. Of course I get annoyed with her acting all insecure and shit, but how can I, when I'm the one who made her that way? I had put her in a situation where I was constantly fuckin' up, and I hated doing that to her.

"Let me use a different approach with you because clearly the one that I've been using isn't going to get us anywhere. Shonte, I'm coming to you right now as a man. Talking to you as the mother of my son and the love of my life, staring you dead in your eyes. You are the one that I want to be with. You are the one I want to carry more of my babies. All the shit that comes with being in a faithful and committed relationship, I want that with you. I'll admit that when we first got together, I wasn't shit, and I wouldn't want a nigga doing half of the shit that I used to do to you to La'shay or my daughter if we had one. With all that being said, you got to trust me, baby. Trust me that I'm going to live up to my word. This ain't the time for us to be beefing right now. We got a bitch out on the loose, probably plotting on us as we speak. She fucked around and caused us to lose our baby, but trust me, there ain't about to be a part two to this shit. Like I told you before, I'm going to get her ass before she can get us," I told Shonte.

I noticed she was still feeling some type of way because she didn't respond.

"You love me?" I asked her, pulling her body closer to mine.

"You know I love you, Jarvis," she finally said.

Indeed, I knew she loved me because most women would have left my black ass already. I always knew Shonte loved me, but that day she came and visited me while I was in prison and she rode the fuck out of my dick in the corner of the visitation room; that shit proved her love, along with a few other things. One of them being that her ass was just as crazy as I was for even agreeing to that shit.

"Remember when you visited me back in prison and I told you how horny I had been in there?" I asked her, which got her to laugh.

"Yeah, when it comes to your ass, I just don't know how to say no. I remember being so scared because I thought that somebody was going to walk past, and then I was going to get arrested too," Shonte said.

This time, she made me laugh. "I could tell your ass was scared. I remember that day to a T. You came in there in this royal blue maxi dress, and it was no way in hell that I could let you walk your ass out of there without fuckin'. I swear that shit felt like heaven that day. Obviously, you didn't know prison code because you had broken one of the most important ones. Whenever a lady came in to see her nigga and she was wearing a dress, we can't let y'all leave without fuckin'," I told her, squeezing her ass tighter. I swear, her shit felt like Jell-O.

"Where you going with this, Jarvis?" she asked me, cocking her head to the side.

"Take a nigga back to that day. Ride me like you did when you came and visited me that day," I said, letting her go and pushing myself back in the chair that I was sitting in.

Shonte quickly went over to my office door, making sure to lock it, and then she came back over to me. She stepped out of the nude Christian Louboutin heels that she was wearing and then removed her tight jeans that almost looked painted on. After she was out of her pants, she pulled the white tank over her head, and now she stood before me in only a black strapless bra and thong.

"Turn around and do that! I want to see that pussy from the back," I told her, once she began to take off her thong.

She seductively turned around, bent over, and touched her toes, giving me a clear view of her pussy. I had just beat that thang up the night before, so her pussy lips were swollen and hanging out of the thong.

With her still bent over, I wheeled myself closer to her in my chair and pulled her thong to the side. I stuck my index finger inside of her, and just like how I suspected, her shit was soaking wet. I pulled the finger out and placed it in my mouth, tasting her juices.

"Damn, that shit tastes good. Let me taste some more, baby, and then you can ride my dick," I told her, pulling her thong all the way down.

Once she stepped out of it, I took her panties and placed them in the pocket of my slacks. With her still bent over touching her toes, I started my tongue from the crack of her ass until I reached her clit.

"Ohhh, Jarvisss," Shonte moaned once I had latched onto her clit and was softly pulling on it between my teeth.

Shonte was a freak for real, so it would turn her little hot ass on whenever I assaulted her clit in a rough manner, like what I was doing now. Using my hands to spread her ass cheeks apart, I went to work on that pussy right there in the middle of my office. I didn't care that I had my crew downstairs, and they could possibly hear the cries that escaped from Shonte's mouth. I used my index finger to slide between her slit, while I continued munching on her pussy from the back. She had her juices all in a nigga's beard and shit.

"Fucccckkkk! Jarvisss, I'm cumm..." she screamed for me.

I started showing off now because I wanted her to cum long and hard. A few seconds later, she let off a big orgasm in my mouth, and I was right there to suck up everything she had to offer. I kissed her thumping clit a few times before I fully sat back in my chair.

"Go ahead. Show is all yours now!" I told Shonte and she turned around.

She bent down to unfasten my slacks, and once she had them down, along with my boxers, she eased her way into my lap and slowly slid down my dick. I held onto her ankles as she began riding my dick nice and slow, exactly how she knew I liked it.

"Like this, daddy?" Shonte paused and squeezed the fuck out of my dick with her pussy muscles. She knew that shit would make a nigga bust quick.

"Don't do that shit, Shonte!" I grunted, but she went against what I said and did it anyways.

I reached up with my right hand and placed it around her neck, chocking her. Not to the point where I was causing pain or anything, but just to let her feel a little bit of this pressure. It didn't matter anyway, because Shonte loved when I manhandled her for some odd reason.

"Ohhh, daddy. I like it when you're rough!" she told me as she continued to bounce up and down on my dick.

She was riding me like she was a damn frog, and each time her ass would slam back into my lap, her pussy would make these farting noises because her shit was so wet. We had our own little groove going on until there were a few knocks at the door.

"Tell them to go away because I'm not stopping until I cum," Shonte whispered to me and then started sucking hard as hell on my neck.

"Jarvis, open the door! I know you in there! I saw your car outside!" La'shay yelled from the other side of the door, fuckin' up the damn mood.

I couldn't even focus right now because Shonte was doing shit to my dick with her pussy that had my head gone. I had to put my hands on her ass to slow her down because I wasn't trying to cum so fast, but clearly she was trying to make me.

"Baby, just cum with me!" Shonte moaned in my ear, squeezing my dick again with her muscles.

She wasn't about to let up, so I let her get this one out of me. Seconds later, we both started cumming together and Shonte crashed her forehead into mine, breathing heavily.

"Damn, I hope that was enough nut to get you pregnant," I said, making her laugh.

I knew we could never replace the child that we lost, but that didn't stop me from wanting to give her more. I had been trying damn near every day to put a baby inside Shonte, but I was still coming up short. Funny how when we both wasn't trying to make a baby, we ended up with Javari, and then the child that we both lost. Now that we were trying, it wasn't happening. Shonte wanted another baby just as bad as I did, which is why she was letting me slide up in her every day, sometimes three times a day.

"Our time will come, Jarvis. Let me go straighten up, and then I'll open the door to see what your sister wants," Shonte said, kissing my lips and then she got up from my lap.

She picked her clothes up from off the floor and then disappeared into the restroom that in my office. Pussy whipped wasn't even the word, as I sat there with visions of the way Shonte just took my dick and forced a nigga up out of his nut a few seconds ago. God, I loved that woman!

# CHAPTER 3

## *Ashanti Palmer*

"God, she's beautiful. Look at all of that hair," my mother cooed as she held onto my baby.

I had just given birth about an hour ago, and I was still weak as hell. Chad and I had decided to name our baby Ariel Williams. Neither Chad nor myself had middle names, so we decided not to give our baby girl one either. Now that the birth was done, I could finally take a minute to myself and just think about the events that led up to this moment. Number one, Chad was not even present for the birth of our baby. Ariel wasn't supposed to come for another two weeks, but she decided to make her grand entrance today.

Earlier this morning, I was home in the den watching TV, when all of a sudden I felt warm fluids seeping out of me. The first thing that crossed my mind was that maybe I was peeing because this wouldn't have been the first time that I had peed on myself since I've been pregnant. But when I stood up and noticed that it was a clear substance coming out of me, I knew then that my water had broken.

In a great amount of pain, with contractions hitting my ass back to back, I called Chad's phone for about twenty minutes straight, but it kept going to voicemail. I ended up having to call my mother. Luckily, she answered the phone on the first ring and was at my house within ten minutes. It was my mother who held my hand, wiped the sweat from my forehead, and even cut the umbilical cord after I had given birth. My mother had done all of the things that my own fuckin' baby daddy wasn't there to do. It wasn't until thirty minutes ago that Chad had finally showed up after I had left numerous messages on his phone, telling him where I would be.

It was his whole vibe that pissed me off when he came into the room. No thank you to me for giving him his first child. No balloons, card, flowers, or anything. All he did was walk over to my mother, who was holding our baby girl, and kiss her on the forehead. Now, he's been sitting in the chair next to my hospital bed, and had yet to say two words to me.

I just didn't understand Chad these days. He acted as if he regretted that him and I ever got together. What hurt me the most is that I knew for a fact that he wishes that I was Shonte. Little comments that he would make to me confirmed that he wanted me to be her. As soon as my mother left, I was going to give him a piece of my mind. I was tired of kissing his ass, when clearly this man didn't give a fuck about me. He showed me that he didn't give a fuck by missing the whole birth, and then strolling his ass in here all late like nothing happened.

Ariel had fallen asleep in my mother's arms, so she picked her up and laid her in the bassinet next to my bed. I knew my mother was ready to get out of this room anyway because she could feel the tension between Chad and I. Knowing her, she didn't want any parts of our drama, and I honestly didn't blame her. After kissing my forehead and telling me to call her if I needed anything, she headed out of the room, closing the door behind her.

"Where have you been, Chad?" I asked calmly as soon as my mother was out of the room.

"My bad, baby. I was out handling business," Chad said, so nonchalantly.

It was as if he could really give two fucks about the way that I was feeling right now. Like the tears in my eyes didn't mean a damn thing to him.

"Your bad? You say that like it's not major. Chad, I came into the hospital at noon. It is now going on nine o'clock at night! You just walked in here no more than thirty minutes ago, so that means that you've been gone and away from your phone for the past eight hours and thirty minutes? On top of that, you walk in here, kiss our daughter on the forehead, and don't even have the balls to say anything to me! I'm not some side chick that you were just fuckin' and I happened to pop up pregnant! You tell me all the time that you love me, yet you come in here and do shit like this. I'm okay with you treating me like shit, but why do the shit in front of my mama, though?" I asked him with tears falling down my face.

I was so fuckin' tired of this man embarrassing me like this. If he didn't want to be with me, that's all he had to say, but I was so fed up with him stringing me along with all of these damn mixed messages.

"You wasn't some side chick that popped up pregnant? Ashanti, did you forget that I was engaged when you and I started fuckin' around? So, to clear your statement up, you most definitely were some side chick I was fuckin' who popped up pregnant. I never planned on having any of this with you. It just fuckin' happened! Sorry, man, but you were just a mistake that went too far. Also, to answer your question that you asked me a few months ago, yes I still love her," Chad told me.

For the first time, I looked into his eyes and I realized that they were red. On top of that, his breath smelled like liquor. I was always told that a drunken mind speaks the truth, so I was glad that it went down this way. Yeah, it hurt to hear this from the first man that I had actually loved, although he was once my best friend's man. To hear him say these things to me cut deeply.

"Funny thing about it is, I know that you and I started off on a lie. We both knew that. When you approached me, wanting to get some revenge on Shonte, I was cool with that. But let's be clear here, we both ended up catching feelings in the end. You told me plenty of times that you loved me, and I believed you until now because if you love a person the way that you say you do, you wouldn't have let that shit fly out of your mouth. I know one thing. I'm tired of accepting shit just to keep a man. A few months ago, I saw on the computer where you had been creeping, looking at Shonte's Facebook page. Me, being so afraid of hearing the truth, I never confronted you about it. I never even said anything to you when you didn't tell your mother about me, let alone that I was pregnant. That goes to show that you're still ashamed of me, probably even ashamed of our baby because you have yet to call your mother and tell her about her granddaughter," I said and then took a deep breath.

I had said what I needed to say to him; what should have been said months ago, but I was too afraid that one wrong word would run him off.

"You don't have a home anymore at my house. Most likely I'll be getting discharged from here tomorrow sometime. When I get home, I want you gone, along with whatever other things that you have over there. You can leave your key as well," I told him.

He sat in the chair and let what I had just told him marinate. If I had learned anything when it came to dealing with men, they were only going to do what a woman allowed them to do. If I continued to turn the other cheek and not speak up to the shit that Chad was doing, he would continue doing it. I loved Chad, but I loved myself more, so therefore I wouldn't allow him to continue playing with my heart like it was a game or some shit.

After sitting there for a few more minutes, he stood up from the chair and made his way to the door. Right now, my focus was on myself and my daughter, fuck everybody else!

# CHAPTER 4

## Shonte Howard

For the first time in my life, I felt like I had to constantly look over my shoulder. Because of Jarvis and his whorish ways, now we had a bitch on the loose, trying to come for myself and my damn family. I'm not even tripping about Jarvis entertaining that bitch that he was messing around with while him and I were apart. At the end of the day, Jarvis had come to me as a man and told me that he didn't want any relationship with me; he just wanted to be there for our son. Yeah, it was hard to accept that, but what the hell could I have done? I'm the one who had hidden a child from him for four years, so there was nothing that I could do or say.

While I may not be mad at him for messing around with another bitch, I'm mad at the type of crazy bitch he decided to fuck with. Any person in their right mind crazy enough to kill their own sister and nephew was a bitch that you had to look over your shoulder for. It's crazy because even on my very first encounter with Malaya, or should I say, Tiffany, she had already rubbed me the wrong way. I don't know what it was about her, but I almost felt as if something was off with her.

Since Jarvis and I found out who she is and what she's capable of, I kept thinking about what could have happened to me that day when she had come into my studio if I didn't have security there. I knew for a fact that she was there for a reason. It's crazy the depths that some women will go to over a man who isn't even theirs. You don't see me going around killing people, and Jarvis is my damn man!

Looking at Malaya, I never would think that she was capable of doing the things that Jarvis and I read about her past or even the things that we assumed that she had something to do with in the present. Even though she did come off as a little weird, she still had this innocence about her.

"What you over there thinking about?" La'shay asked me as she drove and I rode shotgun.

She and I were on our way to my parents' house to pick up Javari. I had been with La'shay since early this morning. We started out at breakfast, worked our way to getting our hair, nails and toes done, and now we were going to pick up my son. I looked over at my best friend of many years, and stared at her for a long time. I was about to confess some shit to her that I haven't said to anyone because I didn't want people to think that I was talking crazy.

"I got to tell you something, but don't tell your brother because him and I aren't supposed to be keeping secrets from each other," I told La'shay.

She nodded her head. "If it's one of your big ass secrets that could cause Jarvis to stop talking to me for a while, then I don't even want to know. Jarvis and my relationship just got back close to how it used to be, and I'm not trying to mess that up again fuckin' around with you," La'shay told me.

I completely agreed with her. I felt so bad when she told me that Jarvis wasn't fuckin' with her either since she was in on the secret that I was holding onto.

"It's not really a secret like that, just more of a confession. Truth is, one of the hardest things for me to do right now is give your brother a baby. I think the reason why it isn't happening is because I'm stressing myself out. La'shay, we talking about a bitch that put a fuckin' dog on me and made me lose the baby that I was just carrying. Don't get me wrong, I'm not scared of the bitch, I'm just scared of getting to the point in my pregnancy where I've already gotten attached to my child, and just that quick, it's taken away from me. That miscarriage was gruesome, and I still get goosebumps every time I go to work and see those damn stairs," I said, shaking my head. Before I blacked out, I remember lying there and seeing all of that blood seeping out of me.

"Shonte, you can't let this bitch have this type of hold on you. Don't let a crazy bitch like Malaya be the reason you're holding back when it comes to giving my brother a child. You're protected, though. Jarvis gave you a gun, so you know to get to busting the first time you lay eyes on that bitch," La'shay said. She made it seem like it was so easy, though.

"Shay, I would lose my mind if that bitch did something to Javari," I told her. Just the thought of that made my voice crack.

"Shonte, don't even talk like that. Why would you even think about some shit like that?" La'shay asked me.

"Because Jarvis and I know that she murdered his other son, Justin, so imagine what the fuck she'll do to Javari!" I snapped.

I didn't mean to raise my voice at La'shay, but I didn't like how she was just waving the situation off, just like like Jarvis was doing.

"Shonte, relax. At the end of the day, you know that when it comes to you and Javari, Jarvis won't let anything happen to y'all, so stop worrying before you stress yourself to death. Live your life, and don't put shit on hold for a bitch like Malaya because it's not even worth the stress," La'shay told me.

I just nodded my head.

About ten minutes later, we pulled up to my parents' house and La'shay parked her car in the driveway. I used the spare key that I had in my purse and let myself in. The moment we walked into the house, whatever my mother was cooking invaded my nostrils, making my stomach growl because I hadn't eaten since this morning.

"Hey, Ma," I said, walking into the kitchen and giving her a peck on the cheek. My mother loved to cook. Whenever she was in the kitchen throwing down, she would have on her custom made apron that had a picture of her and my father on it.

"Hey, baby. Hey, Shay. What the two of you been up to today?" my mom asked me after Shay and I took a seat at the island.

"Nothing much. Where is Javari and Daddy?" I asked her, taking an apple out of the fruit basket and cutting into it.

"Upstairs watching TV," she told me. "Javari, your mom is here," my mom screamed.

A few seconds later, I heard little footsteps coming down the stairs. When Javari reached me, he dived into my arms and I picked him up, sitting him on my lap. I placed kisses all over his face, and that's when I realized that my mom had taken his braids out, and she had my baby's long hair parted down the middle, making him look like a little girl. If Jarvis was around right now to see this, my God, he would have cursed my ass out so bad because he hated when I let Javari wear his hair loose. A lot of times when we would be out in public, Javari's long hair would cause a lot of attention and people would walk up to us saying, "Ohh, she's so cute" or the most popular one, "Ohh, her hair is so pretty." I laughed, thinking about the cursing out that Jarvis would put on them strangers for mistaking our son for a little girl.

"Mommy, why did you take out his braids? You must be trying to get me killed," I told her, putting Javari down and standing up myself. I was about to put the braids back in before I went home to my crazy ass and very controlling baby daddy.

"Because it was time for them braids to come out. You should be thanking my ass. I done took out them damn braids and even washed and blow dried all of that long ass hair. I haven't done no shit like that in years. Hell, since you were a little girl," my mom fussed, causing La'shay to laugh.

No matter how grown I got, my mother would still get in my ass for talking to her crazy and not like the respectful child that she had raised. I would just take it because no matter how old I got, I would never disrespect my mother. I mean, I may cop attitudes here and there, but that's as far as I would go.

While my mom continued to cook dinner, I went into the den area to fix Javari's hair. As soon as I finished, my mom called us to come eat. She made a feast, which consisted of barbeque chicken, yellow rice, collard greens, and blueberry muffins. Thanks to my mom for coming through because Lord knows I didn't feel like cooking tonight.

After we all ate dinner at the table, my mom told me to make a to go plate for Jarvis. La'shay and I stayed back to help clean up the kitchen, and then we left. La'shay dropped me and Javari back to Jarvis' house, and after bathing my son and putting him in his bed, I could now take a shower myself and get in bed as well.

It was Saturday, and I already knew that Jarvis wouldn't be home anytime soon because he had let me know that he was going to the club to celebrate one of his homeboy's birthday. It didn't take long for me to say my prayers, and within minutes, I was knocked out cold.

# CHAPTER 5

## Jarvis Banks

There used to be a time when a nigga couldn't wait to cop a new outfit and slide through King of Diamonds on a Saturday night, just to stunt of all of the broke niggas in the building and to cause a flood in every bitch's draws after they got a look at me. I swear, all of the shit that used to excite me when I was younger, that shit didn't move me anymore. Don't get me wrong, a nigga would never get tired of looking at ass and titties, but damn, I just can't help but to think that I would rather be in bed right now with my girl, making love to her.

Right now, I was in the VIP section of King of Diamonds, celebrating my nigga Devontez's birthday. This nigga was turning thirty, and why he wanted to spend his 30th birthday at K.O.D. was beyond me. I had known Devontez, or should I say Tez, since that's what everybody called him since we were in middle school. Yeah, I was a hot head in school, but this nigga made my ass look like a good boy by the way he would curse teachers and shit out on a daily. He had gotten into so many fights while we were in school, that they eventually kicked his ass out for good.

Tez was one of the students who the teacher would look at and tell him that he wasn't going to be shit in life, but I bet all of them teachers where kicking themselves in the ass right now because Tez was just as successful as I was. Tez had gone on to be a businessman just like myself. This man had over five restaurants in Miami, Atlanta, and New York, and they were all successful. See, the thing about Tez was that he was a smart nigga. Even though he had skipped several grades, I think the classes still weren't challenging enough for him. Once he finished his work, he would go around the class fuckin' with people.

Tez was a good nigga, he was just hood as fuck, and he didn't want to get him one bitch to settle down with. At the end of the day, I know when it comes to women, I wasn't always faithful, but as you grow up, your mindset changes. This nigga was still living life like he was 21 years old, and now that he was turning thirty, he needed to get his life in order.

"Fuck is you so quiet for, nigga? You surrounded by all of this pussy, and you over there nursing that cup of Hennessy, not even fazed by this shit!" Tez said, as he poured more of the Hennessy from his bottle into my cup.

"That's because this shit don't faze me," I told him, making him laugh.

A few minutes later, I noticed my sister walking into our VIP section. I was confused because I didn't even invite her ass with me. I looked behind her to see if Shonte was with her, but she wasn't.

"Fuck you doing here?" I asked La'shay, standing up from the couch and giving her a hug.

I swear I didn't want to let her ass go. The moment I did, I knew these niggas in here were going to be staring at my baby sister with lustful ass eyes because of the shit that she was wearing. La'shay was in a tan fur vest with nothing on underneath, so her breasts were on full display. She had on a tight ass pencil skirt that was high waisted, and a pair of gold heels that she had strapped, going up her legs. I couldn't lie, my sister was beautiful, and I hated to see her growing up on me. The big brother in me made me want to drag her ass by her arm and tell her to take her ass home, but I knew I couldn't do that. Since our father died, I felt like I had to step up and be that male figure in her life, but La'shay would make it clear to me every chance she got that I wasn't her daddy. I wasn't trying to be, though. I was just trying to protect my sister from the evils of this fucked up ass world that we live in.

"Tez invited me. Jarvis, what the hell is wrong with you?" La'shay asked me, laughing because I hadn't let go of her yet.

I finally pulled away from my sister and she was looking at my ass like I was crazy. A few seconds later, she went over and gave Tez a hug. Something about the way she looked at my nigga caused me to raise an eyebrow. First off, she was looking at Tez the same way that I've seen Shonte look at me over a million times. *Damn, was my boy fuckin' my little sister?* I fucked with Tez the long way, but I'll be damned if I allowed him to do my sister dirty the same way that he does these other females out here in these streets. My sister's heart wasn't a fuckin' toy, and I wasn't going to let that nigga treat it as such.

"Nigga, are you seeing this shit, man?" I asked Ki, as I took a seat back on the couch.

"I'm seeing it just like how you seeing it, my nigga. Shay like a sister to me, so I can only imagine how you feeling right now because that's your blood," Kiondre told me.

"At the end of the day, Shay is grown, so what the fuck can I do?" I asked, shaking my head.

"I don't know, man. Talk to him, though. It's probably nothing serious, because if it was, Tez would have told you by now that he was feeling your little sister. As a man, number one, he should have gotten your blessing first and then pursued her," Kiondre let me know, and I couldn't agree with him more.

"The thing about it though, for his case it better be serious because judging by the way my sister is looking at that man, it's pretty serious to her," I said, shaking my head and then standing up.

I couldn't take looking at this shit, so I dapped up Ki, along with the rest of my niggas, and let them know that I would get up with them another time. It was going on one in the morning, so I knew Shonte would most likely be asleep when I made it to the house, but I damn sure was going to wake that ass up and see if she knew anything about my sister messing around with one of my homies. You would think that Shonte would have learned her lesson by now to stop keeping secrets from a nigga, because in the end, I damn sure was going to find out.

After I made it to my car, I jumped behind the wheel and pushed it all the way home. About twenty minutes later, I pulled up to my condo and went to park the car in my usual parking spot.

When I made it into the house, the only light that was on downstairs was the lamp in the den area, which I went and turned off. I walked into the kitchen, saw the plate that was wrapped up in aluminum foil, and assuming it was mine, I placed it in the microwave and warmed it up. All the while, I sat there with thoughts of Tez and my sister on my mind. Damn, La'shay was my baby, and Lord knows I would go fuckin', crazy if a nigga breaks her heart. This was one of the reasons why I was so scared of Shonte giving me a girl because I didn't want a nigga to dog my daughter out the same way that I used to dog her damn mama. I used to do some fucked up shit to Shonte. One of the worst things I used to do was talk to her while I had a bitch in my lap riding the fuck out of my dick, or even while I had a bitch on her knees giving me head. Damn, I hoped karma was good to me because I wouldn't be able to fathom the thought of some shit like that happening to my daughter.

After I had finished eating my food, which was very good by the way, I had a Coke to swallow it all down, and then I made my way upstairs. I went and checked on my son first, making sure he was good. One of the best feelings in the world was coming home to my son after a long ass day. After leaving his room, I walked down the hall and opened the door to the bedroom that I shared with Shonte. She was sprawled out in the middle of the bed, on her back, sleeping in one of my tee shirts. I took a quick shower, and then after throwing on a clean pair of boxers, I climbed in bed with my girl.

Shonte was a light sleeper, so the moving caused her to stir in her sleep. When she saw me sitting up, she jumped, looking at me crazy.

"What time is it?" Shonte asked, looking around.

"It's a little bit after two," I said, pulling her by her arm so that she could lay her head on my chest.

"You had one of them big booty hoes in your lap tonight, giving you lap dances and shit?" Shonte asked, making me laugh.

This girl had no filter when it came to her mouth, and I'll be very grateful when she gets it through her thick ass head that I had eyes for her, and her only.

"What the hell am I going to do with your ass?" I asked, massaging her scalp.

I knew she liked that shit. I had been doing this to her ever since she and I first got together, and she would even do the same thing to our son. A few seconds later, I heard light snoring. I looked down, and that's when I realized that her ass had fallen asleep.

"Shonte, wake up! I need to ask you something," I said. She turned around and laid her head on my lap, looking up at me.

I'm glad she did that because I needed to see her eyes while I asked her this question. Shonte's eyes would tell her soul, so I would know if she was being truthful.

"You knew about Shay messing around with Tez?" I asked her.

"What? Hell no! Shay never mentioned her and Tez messing around to me. How do you even know about this?" Shonte asked, sitting up now.

"Because she came through the club tonight, and judging by the way she was smiling all up in that nigga's face, I already know some shit got to be going down between them. Hell, he even invited her to the club. He was allowing my sister to be all up under him in the club, and ain't no telling how many of his hoes he had in the building tonight," I told Shonte.

"I'm going to ask her tomorrow. It's probably not that deep because Shay tells me everything, and when I say everything, I mean *everything*," Shonte emphasized.

I reached into my nightstand and pulled out a blunt that I was smoking on earlier this morning. Lord knows I needed something to ease my mind after seeing the shit that took place tonight.

"Why you acting like you upset about it, though? Don't you want your sister to be happy?" Shonte asked, forcing me to look at her.

"Yeah, I want my sister to be happy. Fuck you mean? Just not with a nigga like Tez!" I barked at Shonte.

She looked at me and let out a sarcastic laugh. "Fuck you mean with a nigga like Tez? Jarvis, not too long ago your ass was just like him! Don't try and fuck up your sister's happiness because your pride won't let you see your sister be with Tez. How would you feel if back then when I met you, I had somebody in my ear, telling me not to get with you because of the type of nigga that you were?" Shonte asked me.

I was pissed. If anything, I thought she would be on my side because she knew firsthand what it felt like when it came to getting her heart broken.

"I wouldn't have to worry about that because I taught you a long time ago not to listen to shit that you hear people say about me, and you know that!" I told her, taking a long pull from my blunt.

Shonte looked at me, laughed, and shook her head. "Jarvis, your ass just trying to look for a reason to break up some shit. Let Shay be happy. Don't get mad because your sister probably fuckin' now," Shonte told me and laughed, which caused my blood to boil.

I put the blunt out and she tried to jump out of the bed because she knew I was coming for that ass. I grabbed onto her leg, forcing her to lie on her back. When she plopped down, it caused the shirt that she was wearing to rise up. I had a clear view of that fat pussy, since she didn't have any underwear on.

"That shit ain't funny, Shonte, so don't say nothing like that again," I told her, placing both of her arms on top of her head.

"What? Jarvis, we grown, man! Let me go for real because I got to pee," she lied.

I knew damn well her ass ain't have to pee because she would have done that shit the moment she woke up.

"Apologize for what you just said and I'll let you go pee," I told her, dead ass serious.

She laughed at what I just said, all the while trying to get out of the hold that I had her in. "Seriously, Jarvis! Stop playing, man, I got to pee," she whined.

Obviously, she thought this was a joke, so I reached my hands down and started tickling her stomach. I knew for a fact that Shonte's ass was ticklish as hell, so I was only doing this to fuck with her. The whole time I was tickling her, she was laughing hard as hell, kicking her legs at me, and cursing me out at the same damn time.

"Jarviss... wait," she said. I felt some warm shit seeping out of her and it touched my leg.

I shot up out of the bed like my ass was on fire or some shit.

"Fuck is that, girl?" I asked, looking over at Shonte, who had jumped out of the bed as well.

"I told you I had to pee, you asshole!" she snapped at me and then went into the bathroom, slamming the door hard as hell behind her.

I laughed because I couldn't believe this girl had just peed in my damn bed. Oh, I wasn't going to let Shonte live this one down. I was fuckin' with her every day after this. While she did what she had to do in the bathroom, I took the pissy sheets off the bed and replaced them with new ones. By the time I was getting back in the bed, Shonte was walking out of the bathroom. Judging by the look on her face, I already knew she had an attitude with a nigga.

"Damn, you mad, baby?" I asked her the moment she got in the bed.

I pulled her body over to mine. Her back was facing me and I had my arm draped across her, holding onto her breast. Shonte ignored me like I knew she would as I continued to lay kisses on the back of her neck.

"I'm sorry, baby. This our little secret, though. Nobody got to know about your grown ass pissing the bed but you and I," I said, with sarcasm dripping from my voice. I'm sorry, but the shit was funny as hell to me.

"Let's see who's going to be laughing when I don't give your ass no pussy for a whole week!" Shonte snapped back at me.

Just that quick, the smirk that was on my face was completely gone. Wasn't shit funny about her ass holding out on the pussy because she had done it before, and man, it was a fucked up feeling.

"Chill! You ain't even got do all that because I was just fuckin' around with you," I told her.

"Good night, Jarvis," Shonte said, reaching up and turning the lamp off.

True to her word, this woman let me go to sleep tonight with a hard ass dick. Damn, I hope she didn't keep this going for the rest of the week, with her pissy ass!

# CHAPTER 6

## Malaya Brown

*I* was in my bed knocked out cold when all of a sudden, there was some loud ass banging on the front door. Immediately, I got nervous as hell because I thought that maybe it was the police out there banging on the door, waiting to take my crazy ass back to jail. Then again, it couldn't be because I wasn't sloppy with the shit that I had done with my mom's body. It's been about a month since I dumped her body into the river, so I should be straight.

I jumped out of bed and threw on the robe that I had lying on the floor. Placing my feet in my slippers, I walked to the door to see who was banging on my door this damn loud on a fuckin' Saturday morning. When I made it to the door, I looked out of the peephole, and that's when I realized that it was my mother's boyfriend Deon standing at the door. Fuck! I began to panic. I knew for a fact that he was coming over to check on my mom, but sadly for him, my mother's body was thousands of miles away from us right now.

I stood by the door, hoping that he would get the hint and just walk away, but his ass just kept right on knocking. Doing the best thing that I knew to do, I opened my robe little bit, letting my breasts play peekaboo. Hopefully, my body would be enough to distract him.

"Hey," I said, opening the door for Deon.

He quickly fell for the bait because the moment his eyes saw my exposed breasts, it's like he forgot what he even came for. Deon was a handsome guy; he was just not my type at all. I liked me a 'sit the fuck down before I fuck you up' type of nigga. Deon looked like the type of dude who had never used profanity a day in his life. From what my mom told me, Deon worked as an accounts manager down at Bank of America, so most times that I saw him, he was in a suit and tie.

I assume he was off today, since he was dressed casual this morning. Deon looked to be in his early forties, probably the same age as my mother, but he honestly looked good for his age. He had perfect chocolate skin, with some pretty ass white teeth. No tattoos on his body, no flashy jewelry, just your regular working nine to five type of guy.

After clearing his throat, he removed his eyes from my breasts and then looked me in the eyes. "Hey, Malaya. I was just stopping by to check on your mom because it's been about a month since I've heard from her, and that's not like her at all. I've been calling her, but her phone is going straight to voicemail. She's even been ignoring my texts. I called her job and they said that she's hasn't been to work. Do you know where she is?" he asked me with sad puppy dog eyes.

For a quick second, I almost felt bad for his ass.

"Aww man! You didn't hear? My mom had to go to Georgia because my grandmother, her mom, is sick. Her main focus is trying to get my grandmother better because doctors are saying that she had less than a month to live. My grandmother is dying of cancer," I said and my voice cracked.

I forced myself to let tears fall, and a few seconds later, the tears were cascading down my face. "It's just… it's just… my mom works so hard trying to make sure that the people around her are taken care of before she even takes care of herself! It hurts so bad because my mom is up there trying to take care of her, but she called me early today and said that she still isn't getting any better." I cried harder, I even went to the extreme of dropping down to the floor.

"It's okay, Malaya," Deon said, pulling me off the ground and wrapping his arms around me as I continued to fake cry on his shoulder.

Damn, this shit was easier than I thought. Seriously, I was going to have to hit up Tyler Perry or John Singleton because my acting skills were fuckin' top of the line. I needed some type of award for being able to make myself cry at the drop of a dime, and even make it come off as believable too.

"My mom keeps her phone off majority of the day, that's why when you call, it's been going straight to voicemail. She normally doesn't call me until late in the evening, but when she does call today, I'll make sure to tell her that you've been calling her and that you're worried about her," I told Deon the moment I pulled away from his embrace.

"Okay, Malaya. Take care of yourself," he told me and walked away. I watched as he hopped into his Jaguar and pulled off.

Since I was rudely awakened from my sleep, I decided that I may as well get my day started because I had some plotting that I needed to do anyway. My goal for today was to find out where Jarvis and his bitch rested their heads. Once I found out, boy was I about to make their life a living hell. After showering and throwing on some clothes, I went into the kitchen, grabbed a plastic bag from up under the kitchen counter, and I started filling it up with all types of snacks. Trust me, I was going to need it.

I grabbed my purse and the keys to my mom's car, which I had pretty much made mine. Hell, I had made this house mine overnight as well. See, the thing is, this house used to be my grandparents' house, so when they died, they left it to my mother since she was their only child. If I knew that by killing my mom I was going to get my own car and house, I would have taken that bitch out a long time ago. Then again, no I wouldn't because my mom and I used to be so close, but I noticed the change in her when I got back from the mental institution. It was almost as if she was ashamed of me, but she never spoke up on it, though. Then, after everything went down with my sister and Justin, I could see it in her eyes that she hated my ass and she knew I was guilty.

I may try to act big and bad all the time, but it kind of bothered me that I had no one right now. There wasn't a friend that I could hit up right now to go out later on for drinks because the friends that I did have down here in Miami didn't fuck with me like that after I killed Tank. Besides, who the fuck wanted to be friends with somebody as fucked up as myself? How can you be around somebody as heartless as me? The only friend that I could truly say that I had was my sister, and it's too late because she's dead and I'm the reason for it. Mya was a friend to me before anything because she was the only person who never really judged me when I killed Tank. Well, at least she didn't say the shit to my face. If anything, she pushed me every chance she got to take my medicine, even if it would annoy the hell out of me.

As I was driving, I noticed that a tear had fallen from my eyes. Not a fake tear either, this was some real shit. It felt kind of weird because I hadn't cried in years. I honestly couldn't even remember the last time that I had cried. Quickly wiping the tears from my face, I continued on to my destination. About ten minutes later, I found myself in the parking lot of the plaza where Shonte's studio was located. So many times, I had this crazy idea of setting her building on fire because I knew that would piss her off for sure, but I felt like that was too common. I wanted to take this bitch out with a bang. Muthafuckas set buildings on fire every day, I wanted to do something special with her ass. Besides, if I set the shit on fire today, Jarvis would have her spoiled ass with an even bigger space by tomorrow. At the end of the day, I would still lose.

Just like when I fucked up her pretty ass Mercedes jeep at the mall that day. Clearly I had lost that one because now, parked in the owner's parking space was a brand new Bronze colored Bentley truck. I had to admit, that shit was beautiful.

I found a parking spot in the back of the lot, mainly because the lot was full and I didn't want to look suspicious. Seconds turned into minutes and the minutes turned into hours as I stayed camped out in my car, waiting for Shonte to bring her ass out. I got there at eleven o'clock in the morning, and it wasn't until eight in the evening that she finally brought her ass out of the studio. They treated this bitch like royalty as security escorted her to her car.

About two minutes later, she started her car up and I followed right behind her. Once we got onto the main road, I made sure to stay at least one car behind her because I wasn't trying to blow my cover. About ten minutes later, she turned into a housing community out in Miramar. I stayed at the front of the development because I saw when she continued to drive straight and then she finally turned her car into the driveway of a home. I drove a little further down, parked my car and watched her. I assumed this wasn't her home because she got out and left the car running.

A few minutes later, she walked out of the house carrying her handsome baby boy, who was asleep in her arms, while an older man walked behind her carrying her son's book bag. *Ohhhh, so this must be the bitch's parents' house!*

After she placed the baby in the back seat, she kissed her father on the cheek and then she pulled off. That was my cue to take off as well because this bitch drove fast as hell, and it was kind of hard to keep up with her ass. We made it back onto the main road, and every time she switched, I would switch. When she slowed down, I slowed down. I got a little confused when this bitch made a U-turn and headed back in the direction of her parents' house.

"What the fuck is this bitch doing?" I asked myself.

A few minutes later, we pulled back into the same housing community that we had just come out of. I figured maybe the baby must have left something, but I was even more confused when she carried him back into the house, and came back empty handed. When she got back in the car, I waited a few more seconds and then pulled off after her.

# CHAPTER 7

## Shonte Howard

*I* wasn't the smartest bitch in the world, but it didn't take a rocket scientist to know that I was being followed. My intuition really began to kick in right after I picked my baby up from my parents' house, and when I pulled out, I noticed that the Honda parked a few houses down had pulled out as well. At first I thought maybe I was just tripping, but when I started purposely switching lanes and shit, I noticed that the car was doing the same. I knew then that I was being followed for sure, and I knew it was by a bitch because when I hit that U-turn to take my baby back to my parents, I saw a glimpse of burgundy hair.

I couldn't look at the figure for a long time because I had my baby in the backseat and I needed to focus on the road. I was confused as hell because I didn't know any bitch with burgundy hair other than myself and no one who drove a white Honda at all.

When I got back to my parents' house, I dropped Javari back off, lying and telling them that I had to pick La'shay up from the club since she was drunk, and that I didn't want Javari to see her that way. Shit,

I know it didn't make sense, I just needed to come up with something quick, fast, and in a hurry because I was damn sure about to find out who in the hell was following me.

After dropping my baby off, I jumped back on the main road, pushing 90 miles in this beautiful ass Bentley truck that Jarvis had purchased for me a few weeks ago. This car was so fuckin' beautiful that I didn't even want to drive my Mercedes truck anymore.

About ten minutes later, we pulled up to Scott Lake Park out in Miami Gardens. I wanted to see if whoever was behind the wheel would fall for the bait, and sure enough, they did because now it was just the two of us in the parking lot.

I reached in the backseat and grabbed my purse, taking the gun out and placing it in the waist of my jeans before I got out of the car. Jarvis would probably kill my ass dead right now if he knew what I was out here doing, but I honestly didn't care. I just wanted to see who in the fuck was following me. Walking over to the car, I banged on the driver's window with the palm of my hand. A few seconds later, the window came down and I got the shock of my life to see Malaya.

I was amused at this shit, so I let out a sarcastic laugh, even though what I really wanted to do was pull out my gun and kill this bitch. "Should I refer to you as Tiffany, Melissa, or Malaya?" I asked her, cocking my head to the side.

"Refer to me as the bitch who's going to steal your fine ass baby daddy away from you!" she shot back at me.

It was then that I realized that the smile I always saw her wearing wasn't as genuine as I thought it to be. I laughed at what she said because bitches had been telling me for years that they were going to steal Jarvis from me, and I was still waiting for that day to come.

"Bitch, you had plenty of time to take my baby daddy away from me, but clearly you can't take a man that's already kept! Bitches like you fuckin' kill me! What's your motive, though? Fuck you following me around for?" I asked her, cocking my head to the side.

I took in her appearance, and when I realized what she had done, I laughed right in her face. "That's what's different about you! Hoe, you want to be me so bad that you really went and dyed your hair the same color as mine! I read that news article about your psychotic ass, but I thought they was bullshitting when they labeled you insane! Bitch, your ass really is crazy!" I told her.

I must have struck a nerve because she swung the door open so hard that it knocked me right on my ass. But as quickly as I fell, I got back up.

"Too bad you didn't get up that quick when I put that dog on your ass!" Malaya said.

She released a sinister laugh that pissed me off so bad that I just punched her ass dead in her mouth.

"Yeah, but the same nigga you doing all of this over is trying to put another one up in me every night!" I said, punching her ass again.

We went at it in the middle of the parking lot, fighting like two niggas on the fuckin' street. I ain't even going to lie, she got my ass good in my eye, which only enraged me even more. Right now, I was on top of her, landing blows quick as hell to that face of hers. As I was fucking her up, I was just thinking about a lot of different shit, but the main one being that this was the bitch who had caused me to miscarry.

"I'll kill your ass before I let you come near me or my family!" I told her with both of my hands wrapped around her neck, trying to strangle her to death.

I was sitting on top of her and she was trying her best to pry my hands from around her neck, but it was like I had blacked out or something. When I saw her body stop moving and her eyes roll to the back of her head, I panicked. I didn't know if she was dead or not, and honestly I didn't want to stick around and find out. When I got into my car, my body was trembling something serious. *Did I just commit my first murder?*

As I pulled off, I looked at my phone and noticed that I had over ten missed calls from Jarvis. I didn't have what it took to talk to him right now, so I opted not to call him back. Seeing Malaya's eyes roll like that to the back of her head had my ass spooked for sure.

I finally made it home, and when I did, Jarvis' car was parked. He was about to get in my ass, I already knew. I parked the car in my usual parking space and got out, grabbing my purse with me. It felt like every bone in my damn body was broken after doing all of that rolling around on that fuckin' concrete. I used my key and let myself into the house then I set my purse down on the table. Kicking my shoes off by the door, I followed the smell of weed smoke to the den area.

Jarvis was sitting up in his chair, that he didn't allow anyone to sit in other than himself, with his feet propped up. He seemed to be without a care in the world, but I knew that he was pissed as hell right now. He was in a white tank top that had his muscles and tattoos on full display, with a pair of Nike shorts on. His bald head was shining due to the light that was over him, and his goatee was trimmed to perfection. No lie, Jarvis was fine as hell, but I honestly was afraid to be around his ass right now.

"Fuck you been? And why wasn't you answering your damn phone while I was calling you? Most importantly, where the hell is my son?" Jarvis asked me.

I stood there playing with my fingers, because for one, I was scared as shit, and on top of that, I now had to confess to him the shit that I had just done. He took a long pull from the blunt and then he turned around and looked at me. My white outfit was now dirty as hell, with both Malaya's blood and mine on it. On top of that, my eye was a little swollen, and I had a deep gash under it from falling face first onto the concrete. I had other little cuts and bruises on my arms as well.

The moment Jarvis got a clear view of my face, he put the joint out and then jumped up quick as hell. He tried to grab my chin, but I kept trying to fight him off of me.

"Be still! Who the fuck did this shit, yo?" he asked me.

I could tell that he was pissed the hell off, which I knew for a fact that he would be. I ran down the story to him and when I was done, he shook his head at me in disappointment.

"Oh, so I give you a fuckin' gun, and now all of a sudden you a badass? Suppose when you got out of the car, you were being followed by some niggas and they grabbed your little pretty ass up, ran a train on you, and then killed your ass? Huh? That shit didn't cross your fuckin' mind, did it?" Jarvis barked at me.

He was so mad that spit was flying out of his mouth the entire time that he talked to me. I don't even think he was this mad with me when he came face to face with Javari that day at La'shay's house for the first time

"But I knew it was a female, Jarvis, because I saw the hair!" I yelled at him.

"What the fuck does that mean, Shonte? You saw one person, how you know it wasn't other people in the fuckin' car? You should have never gotten your ass out the damn car to begin with. If you knew for a fact that somebody was following your ass, why wouldn't you just pick up the phone and call me? You know I drop everything when it comes to you!" Jarvis yelled, and then he went over and slipped on his Nike slides, along with his keys.

"Where you going?" I asked him, but he ignored me.

Fuck that, I was about to go with his ass. I followed him out to his car, and surprisingly, he didn't tell me to take my ass in the house. We jumped into his truck and he floored it, not even giving me the chance to close the door all the way before he took off. The whole way there to wherever we were going, I kept asking him where the hell he was taking us and he kept ignoring me. Every time Jarvis ran into a red light, he would turn the light on in the car, examine my face once again, and then shake his head.

Fifteen minutes later, we pulled back up to Scott Lake park. Jarvis parked his car in the parking lot and then turned to look at me.

"I left her right there," I said, pointing my finger to where I had last seen Malaya. "And her car was parked over there," I said, pointing to the back of the parking lot. Malaya's car was gone, and so was her body.

"Well, the bitch ain't here, man!" Jarvis said and then he pulled out of the parking lot.

Damn, this shit was starting to feel like them damn Lifetime movies that I love to watch. There was literally no trace of Malaya at this damn park!

# CHAPTER 8

## *Ashanti Palmer*

*I* meant what I said when I told Chad back at the hospital to get his shit out of my home and to leave his key. At first he clearly took me for a joke because when my mother brought me home the next day from the hospital, he was in the living room knocked out cold on the couch. Ariel was asleep, so I took her upstairs to her room and laid her down in her very own bed for the first time.

Once I made sure that baby girl was alright, I headed back downstairs to wake Chad's ass up and tell him to get the fuck out of my house. I hated the fact that I was so stupid when it came to him, because now it was one whole month later, and I still had his ass living here with me. Only difference was that we weren't sharing the same room, and he was now going half with me on the bills, which is what he should have been doing in the beginning. Wasn't no way in hell I was about to continue taking care of a disrespectful ass nigga for free. So, basically, Chad and I were just roommates, but I'll admit that he was indeed a big help when it came to Ariel. We both had baby monitors in our room so we would alternate on waking up in the middle of the night when she cried.

As far as Chad and I getting back together, I honestly didn't know if that was going to happen because I felt like the only reason why he was trying to get back into my good graces is because he was afraid that I would kick his ass out. Let's be real, that little part time job that he had at UPS wasn't enough for him to get his own apartment, so his ass needed me!

It had been a month since I had the baby, and I was ready to get back to work. I knew the day was going to come that I would have to go on maternity leave from the barbershop, which is why I had been saving up from the moment I found out that I was pregnant. My savings were beginning to get a little light, so I needed to take my ass back to work. Luckily, my mother told me that she didn't have a problem at all watching my baby while I worked. So, right now, I was headed outside to my car, about to take my baby over to my mom's and then I was off to work, after being gone for over two months. I was thankful for snapping right back into shape after I had Ariel, but I was still trying to get my stomach back to its washboard self before I had the baby.

Around noon, I pulled up to the shop and it was busy as usual. I parked my car and then grabbed my bags and walked into the building. Ki was the first person I saw when I walked in. Since this was his shop, his booth was the first one, right when you walked in. For some reason, I was expecting him to be excited to see me since I made him a lot of money by being one of the best female braiders here in Miami, but all I got from him was a dry, "hey". It didn't take a rocket scientist to know that Shonte had probably got in his ear about the shit that I had done.

Now he was looking at me funny, which is to be expected. Shonte is like a little sister to him, so his loyalty lied with her.

Aside from him, everybody else was happy as hell to see me. It didn't take long for me to start taking customers back to back, and before I knew it, my smock was filling up quickly with money.

Around 3 o'clock, the door opened and I noticed Jarvis walk in. I got so scared because I thought he had Shonte with him, but thankfully, for my sake, he was alone. I breathed a sigh of relief because I already knew that the moment Shonte saw me, she was going to lay hands on me. I mean, the bitch tried to take my fuckin' head off while I was pregnant, so imagine the shit she'll do now that I'm not?

Jarvis' eyes met mine and then he shook his head before walking over to me. I already knew that he was about to come over here on some bullshit, so I mentally prepared myself for it.

"Damn, what you gon' do to make me not call my baby mama up here to beat your ass? She not going to rest until she lay some hands on you," Jarvis said to me.

I ignored him as I continued to put braids in the man's hair that I was doing.

"The way you get him is the way you lose him. Remember that, lil mama," Jarvis told me and then he went back over and finished talking with Kiondre.

I let what he said to me sink in, and wondered if Chad had another bitch that he was entertaining.

# CHAPTER 9

## La'shay Banks

*I*t was three in the morning and I was laid up on my back in Tez's bed, and the only sound that could be heard in his room was his constant snoring, mixed with his phone that kept vibrating on his nightstand nonstop. Certain moves Tez would make, most times I wouldn't speak on it because I already knew how he got down when I opened up my legs for him. Besides, it wasn't enough to make me leave this man alone.

Before I even get on how Tez and I first started fuckin' around, let me start from the very beginning of who La'shay really is. I've never been the girl who was interested in boys like that because when I was younger and Jarvis used to live with us, I watched the way that he treated girls. This was way before Jarvis and Shonte even hooked up. In fact, I didn't even know Shonte yet because she and I didn't meet until high school. I remember being in elementary and middle school, and Jarvis used to have all type of girls calling the house phone looking for his ass.

Whenever he would eventually answer the phone for them,

he would have to ask them to state their name because his hoe ass wouldn't even know who he was talking to at the time. I was seeing shit like this at about ten years old, and I remember thinking that all boys were like my brother. So, while most girls were interested in boys and shit in middle school, that was the furthest thing from my damn mind. I remember thinking to myself that I would never want to be one of those girls, calling and looking for a dude who didn't want shit to do with me, but it was something about Devontez that I couldn't resist. I wish I didn't love his ass so much because he was no good for me.

Devontez had been around for a long time because him and my brother were very close. He used to come over to our house when we were younger, and I would sit in my room and watch Jarvis and him as they hung out in the front room, talking, playing the game, or whatever else they were doing. Nobody, not even my best friend, Shonte, who I told everything to knew about my crush on Devontez. I guess I was a little bit ashamed to admit that I liked him because I didn't want people to think that I was crazy to be liking Tez's ass out of everybody. Even when we were younger, Devontez was a little player. On top of that, he was bad as hell, so I knew for a fact that any parent in their right mind wouldn't want their daughter involved with him.

You see, Devontez grew up in a household with just himself and his two brothers, Farrell, and his other brother, Khyree, who was murdered two years ago. But before Khyree was killed, he along with his two brothers, all treated women the same, which was in a disrespectful manner. I don't care what nobody says, I think the reason why the three of them didn't know how to treat women is because they didn't have a male figure in their life while they were growing up to treat their mother the correct way.

I know you may be wondering, why the hell are you laid up with this man if you know for a fact that he is a hoe and that he is disrespectful as hell to women? Truth is, I can't help but to love Tez. I mean, when he's on his best behavior, he treats me like a fuckin' princess. I wasn't with Tez for his money though; I was with him because I know for a fact that he didn't know how it felt to be loved, so I wanted to be the first person to love him. I hated that this had to sound like the typical black man's story.

Growing up, their mother used to abuse drugs, her favorite one being cocaine. She slacked in her position as a mother, which is why Tez showed out so badly in school. Now, fast forward almost fifteen years later, and Tez was a fuckin' businessman; a suit and tie wearing ass nigga that I just couldn't seem to get enough of. Even with all of that, I still couldn't get this nigga to keep that good dick in his pants. The only dick that I ever had. Call me stupid, but I made up my mind a long time ago that I was saving myself for him, and my dumb ass had done it too.

Not able to take the constant vibrating anymore, I got up from my side of the bed to get his phone. I hated that I was looking like some weak, insecure bitch, checking phones and shit, but desperate times call for desperate measures. I knew the password to Tez's phone because I had seen him type it in numerous times. As soon as I was able to unlock it, numerous texts from different bitches popped up in his phone. Most of the women were asking him questions like when was he going to come over and there were even picture messages in his phone of bitches sending him nudes.

I got so damn mad that I just threw the phone at him and it clocked him right in his fuckin' head, instantly waking him up. Like the true hood nigga that Tez was, he grabbed the gun that he kept up under his pillow and pointed it at me. I screamed to let him know that it was me who was standing there, and he lowered the gun.

"The fuck is you doing, Shay? And why would you throw that damn phone at a nigga?" Tez asked me, pulling the cover off of him.

I stood there and looked at this nigga, shaking my head at myself because I was tired of him hurting me, and me letting him get away with the shit. Tez was fine as hell, I'm not even going to lie. His skin tone is what most would consider to be high yellow, and he had good ass hair because his mother was mixed with Cuban. He had these light gray eyes that I couldn't get enough of, but it was the tattoos adorning his body that drove a bitch crazy. Tez had permanent gold fangs on the top row of his teeth, and he kept his hair cut low, with his waves on swim. Tez stood about a good 6'3" and he was pure muscle. That's because him and my brother worked out damn near every day, and the shit had paid off.

I used to let Tez get away with certain shit that he was doing to me, but my feelings were getting deeper involved, and I can't allow him to keep hurting and disrespecting me like this. He was the reason why I didn't tell anybody that I was fuckin with him because I was scared of the way that he would embarrass me out here in these streets. I've seen bitches approach Shonte, and I didn't have time for that.

"What was all that shit you was telling me the other night, Tez?

You told me last night that you were going to start being faithful and that I didn't have to worry about you fuckin' with these random ass bitches anymore! Let me guess, you were just feeding my ass a bunch of bullshit ass lies because you had me on my back and your dick was buried inside of me!" I told him.

I was so mad about seeing the picture message in his phone, that I jumped on him, laying all types of punches to his face.

"Ay! Calm your ass the fuck down!" Tez barked at me, slamming me onto my back and holding my arms on either side of my body. Them little hits that I was putting on his ass clearly didn't move him because he didn't seem to be hurting.

"Do I put my fuckin' hands on you? No the fuck I do not, so don't put your hands on me, Shay. Fuck was you going through my phone for anyway?" he asked, grilling me.

"You don't have to fuckin' put your hands on me, your actions hurt me enough! Move, get the fuck off of me!" I screamed, kicking my legs, trying to knee him in the nuts, but he dodged it.

In the middle of all this, his phone was still vibrating behind me and picked it up, since it was right by my head. I don't know how I was able to get out of his hold, but I damn sure did. I looked at the caller's name and it read "Lil freak Jada". Shaking my head, I answered the phone, all while Tez was trying to get it out of my hand.

"Hello?" I said with an attitude and out of breath.

"Umm, where my man Tez at?" the ghetto bitch asked me.

"If he was your man, wouldn't you be with him right now, and wouldn't you know about his fuckin' whereabouts?" I snapped.

"Bitch, Tez know you got his phone?" she asked, laughing at me.

I guess I wasn't the only one who knew that Tez didn't play that shit about people touching his phone, with his cheating ass. This nigga could go to the bathroom to take a piss, and he would make sure to take that damn phone with him. If him and I went to the gas station and he had to go inside and left me in the car, he took that damn phone. Even if I was around him, he always kept his phone face down. This nigga acted like he held the key to the damn White House in the damn phone the way he carried on.

Snatching the phone from me, Tez but the phone to his ear. "Who this?" he barked at the bitch over the phone. "Yeah, that was my girl. Ay, watch your fuckin' mouth when it comes to that one because I'll have you picking up your fuckin' jaw off the floor," Tez barked out to her.

One thing about Tez, he wouldn't allow a nigga or a bitch to disrespect me, even if I was in the wrong. Yet, his stupid ass would disrespect me all of the fuckin' time. After hearing enough of him talking to that bitch, I jumped out the bed and went into his bathroom. I quickly took a piss and then went over to the sink, brushed my teeth, washed my face and threw my hair up into a bun. I walked back into the bedroom in only my bra and panties, looking for the clothes that I had come over there with the other night. The whole time, Tez sat there smoking, as if nothing had just gone down.

"Let me guess. You running again?" Tez asked me.

"Fuck you, Tez! I'm so sick of this shit. Whatever it is that you and I have going on, I can't continue to do this shit to myself, man! You don't give a fuck about me, and I'm tired of trying to convince myself that you do!" I screamed. I found my jeans on his side of the room and I slid them up my body.

"Ohh, so I don't give a fuck about you, that's what you saying? That pretty ass Porsche that you pushing, who the fuck bought you that shit? Who paying rent over there in them fancy ass condos that you staying at? Don't I come over there every night, drop dick off in you, and I always leave your ass with money? Who paying your tuition right now for you to go back to school and get your bachelors? You don't even got to work, Shay, because I take good care of your ass, yet you insist on working. If it's anybody's fault why we ain't staying together it's yours because you too scared to move in with a nigga!" Tez said to me.

Yeah, everything Tez said was true, but it still didn't make up for all of the other fucked up shit that he did to me.

"Tez, look at what the fuck just happened between us, that's the fuckin' reason why I haven't moved my ass up in here with you! A bitch couldn't even get any sleep without your phone going off back to back in the middle of the fuckin' night!" I screamed at him.

Damn, this nigga sure knew how to piss a bitch off. At times like this, I wish that I could be open about me and Tez's relationship to Jarvis, so that my brother could talk some sense into his ass. I knew Jarvis wouldn't agree with me dating his friend, which is why I had opted not to tell him. Jarvis wasn't one of those controlling ass big brothers, but I'll be damned if his opinion didn't matter to me. Plus, I couldn't even get Tez to act right, so why in the hell would I go around telling people about our relations?

"You might as well sit the fuck down because you ain't going nowhere, Shay. Take your ass to sleep or something!" Tez told me as I continued looking for my shirt.

I bent down on the floor, looking up under the bed and that's when I spotted it. I grabbed the Armani Exchange shirt off the floor and pulled it over my head.

"Walk out that damn door and see what I do to your ass! That's your fuckin' problem right there, La'shay. You take a nigga for a muthafuckin' joke! You think I'm all bark and no bite, but let's see how bad you really are!" he told me.

I continued to ignore his little threats. Tez made threats all the time and they fell on deaf ears, just like how they were doing now. Once I found my Michael Kors flip flops, I grabbed my Birkin Bag off the dresser and walked out of his room. I took the spiral staircase, and when I reached the front door, I could hear Tez coming behind me. My fingers shook as I unlocked the door. Once I got it to open, I hightailed out of there.

I fumbled in my purse for my keys, and the moment I found them, Tez grabbed me up from behind, slamming me onto the hood of his car. Here we were outside at damn near three in the morning, probably waking up his neighbors and shit with all of this noise. I looked up at him with tears welled up in my eyes; not because I was scared, but because I was hurting, and he was the cause of it.

"Tez, just let me go home. I can't keep doing this shit with you!" I told him as the tears that I was trying to hold in spilled out of my eyes.

He didn't even answer me. He just lifted me up off of the car and carried me back into his house. Once he got me back into his room, he laid me down on my back, bent down and removed my shoes, my jeans and my top. I just lay there and allowed him to do it. Once he had me completely naked, he got in the bed with me, pulled my body close to his and held me tight.

"This shit ain't gon' happen overnight, Shay. It's like you always fussing about the bad shit that I do to you, but what about the good? I'm fuckin' trying, man. I ain't never in my life tell another woman that I loved them, not even my mama, but I love the fuck out of you, man. Don't be so quick to throw in the towel, yo," Tez said, kissing my neck.

The whole time he talked to me, I had tears falling down my face because this was the first time that he had told me that he loved me. I knew I should have stopped him when he did it, but I was so weak for him that I couldn't. So, as we lay in bed together, he used his index finger and finger fucked me nice and slow as his thumb massaged my clit. The way he was sucking on my neck hard as hell and whispering sweet nothings in my ear had my body going crazy.

"Shittttt… Tezzz… Imma cummmm…" I said slowly.

My voice got caught right in the middle of my throat because the second I came, I felt his big dick slide up inside me from the back. Usually when Tez and I had sex, we went at it hard and rough. I'm talking choking, the whole nine. The last time I remember Tez being this gentle with me is when he popped my cherry a few months ago. Tonight was so different from all the other times because he kept telling me he loved me, and for some reason, I believed him!

# CHAPTER 10

## Deon Hilton

Something about what Malaya told me the last time I was over there asking about Teresa that had me second guessing everything that she said. Well, for starters, Teresa and I had been together for about a year now, and she never went a day without texting or calling me. It wasn't until a whole month had gone by that I realized I hadn't heard from her, which was the only reason why I decided to pop up at her house.

I was giving her space because I knew that she had been going through it ever since the murder of her daughter and her grandson. When it happened, she had told me that she needed a break from our relationship, and I understood that. I mean, no mother should have to bury her child and grandchild at the same time, so I never complained. I loved the hell out of Teresa, and I missed her company. Plus, I wanted to be the one to hold her while she was mourning. I knew that I had to pop up that day and check on her.

It had been about a month since I went to the house and had that conversation with Malaya, and I realized that what she had told me was a lie. The day I saw Malaya, I'll admit that I was a little taken aback by her standing before me with her breasts showing, and I couldn't think straight. But now, a whole month later, I realized that when Teresa and I first got together, she informed me that both of her parents had died years ago. So, how is it that she's in Atlanta right now taking care of her sick mother? Most importantly, what was Malaya trying to hide that she wouldn't allow me to see Teresa?

It was going on one o'clock in the morning, and I was camped outside about four houses down from Teresa's house, waiting for the perfect opportunity to go inside.

It was now about that time because I had just witnessed Malaya pull her car out of the garage and shoot down the street. Earlier today, I had found a spare key to Theresa's house, so I was going to use that to let myself in. I kept my car parked at the vacant house and I got out. When I reached the front door, I pulled out the key and let myself in. Walking around the house, nothing looked out of the ordinary. I walked to Theresa's room and there her phone was, sitting right on her nightstand. I noticed that there was a folded up piece of paper on her dresser, so I went over and opened it.

*If anybody is reading this letter, it's probably because I didn't make it out alive. Whoever is reading this, please call the police and let them know that I was murdered by my daughter, Malaya Brown, and that I have strong reason to believe she is the one who murdered her sister Mya and nephew Justin Brown.*

"You just couldn't stay away huh, Deon?" I heard a voice say.

I looked up in the doorway and there stood Malaya in the flesh, with her gun trained on me. "Whatever you had planned, you would have almost gotten away with it. But the fact that you sat your ass in your car in the wee hours of the morning with your high beams on gave it away! Everything you saw before you came in here, I wanted you to see! I never left. I backed out of the garage, went up the block and I watched you get out of your car and come into this house. Damn, was my mother's pussy that good that you're willing to die over it?" she asked me as she kept the gun trained on me.

"What did you do to her?" I asked, standing up from the bed and putting the note back down. I wanted to keep her talking, that way I could find a way to get that gun out of her hand. That was the only advantage she had over me. Without that gun, she wasn't shit.

"Do you want to know full details or the short version?" she asked, releasing a sinister laugh.

Damn, so all that talk Teresa was telling me about Malaya being crazy was true, because it honestly felt like I was standing face to face right now with the damn devil. Noticing that she wasn't going to get an answer out of me, she decided to fill me in anyway.

"She was going to kill me, but I killed her first. I had to have stabbed her about twenty times," she told me.

Hearing her say that caused me to lose control. When I lunged at her, she shot the gun, hitting me once in the chest but I still kept charging, trying my best to fight through the pain. I had to fight for Mya, Teresa, and Justin. She let the gun go off again, this time, hitting me twice in both knee caps, instantly sending my body to the floor. I looked up at her as blood seeped out of my body. She stood over me with the gun pointed directly at my forehead.

"You should have just let it go. See where being nosy gets you?" she said.

*Pow! Pow! Pow! Pow!* And it was lights out for me.

# CHAPTER 11

## Shonte Howard

Today was the big day. In about two more hours, we were about to be on our way to Extreme Action Park in Fort Lauderdale to celebrate Javari's 5th birthday. I couldn't believe that it's already been five years since I was in the hospital giving birth, and being in the most pain that I had ever experienced in my entire life. Jarvis was so excited about today because this was his first time getting to spend a birthday with Javari, so you already know Jarvis was going overboard with the gifts, even though our son didn't need shit else.

I was convinced that if Jarvis could, he would have bought our son a damned car. I had been up since six this damn morning because Javari came in here bright and early, wanting to know where his gifts were. I was already exhausted because the night before, I was up by myself putting together candy bags for all of the kids. I swear I was going to need me a damn drink to get through the day.

It was finally that time, and myself, my son, and Jarvis were pulling up to the park. Of course, we were over forty-five minutes late. My son looked so handsome that I had to keep snapping pictures of him before we left. He was in a black custom made shirt with a picture of him with the words Birthday Boy and had the number five on it with a pair of black True Religion jeans and some all black huaraches. Jarvis had even gone so far as buying Javari a little Cuban link to go around his neck. Right now, my son was looking like one of those Instagram babies that you see online.

Jarvis had the same outfit on as our son. Mine was similar, but my shirt was a tank with my son's picture and I had on a pair of black True Religion shorts that were ripped at the bottom. I'm surprised as hell that Jarvis let me come out of the house with them on because they were extremely short. This was Miami, and we were in the middle of the summer, so it was shorts and sundresses until this damn heat slowed down. I also had on a pair of crispy, black low top Converse, and my burgundy hair was perfectly feathered to perfection after getting it styled yesterday.

"Damn, it's about time. How the fuck y'all going to be late at your own damn son's event?" Kiondre asked, walking over to us and taking the box that I had in my hands with the candy bags.

It was a full house, and Javari had disappeared to be with his friends from school. For Javari to only be in kindergarten, he sure had a lot of damn friends here. I stood off to the side and watched as the little girls tugged Javari's arm and played with his hair. As a mother, it made me get a little teary eyed because Lord knows I wasn't ready for the day that my son would grow up and start dating. Hell no! Javari was my baby; always would be, and the idea of a girl one day coming into his life and taking up the majority of his time didn't sit right with me.

I laughed to myself, thinking about how I knew for a fact that my son's girlfriend or whoever the hell he brought around would hate my damn guts because I would not make it easy for them when it comes to dating my son. I decided to shrug those ill feelings off because I knew that day wouldn't come anytime soon.

Jarvis and I went around the room speaking to everybody, and then I went and took a seat next to La'shay. I looked at her and paid attention to what had her focus. She was shooting daggers across the room at Tez as he stood over with the rest of the men. I'll admit, Tez was fine as fuck. I mean, the type of fine that would have any bitch that was fuckin' him wanting to stalk his ass throughout the day and see what the hell he was doing. I think it was the good eyes, the good hair, and all of the tats that drove women crazy.

"That look is all too familiar. The nigga done fucked you good and now he fuckin' up?" I said to Shay with a smirk on my face.

"I swear his ass gets on my damn nerves," La'shay told me, making me laugh.

That look she was giving him was very familiar. I knew exactly how it felt to be in a room filled with people and be annoyed as hell with your man. But you have to chill and act like everything is okay, so you don't nut up in front of everybody. Whatever it was that Tez had done, it had to be to the extreme because Shay looked fuckin' pissed.

"And when the hell were you going to tell me that you and Tez were fuckin' around?" I asked her, taking a sip from the bottled water that I had in my hand.

"This is the reason why I didn't tell you, Shonte! Because his ass has some fuckin' whorish ways, so I wasn't ready to tell you yet," she told me with this scowl on her face.

"What? You thought I was going to judge you or some shit? I'm in no position to talk down on any woman when it comes to who they're dating, especially because of all the bullshit that I endured fuckin' around with your brother. I don't even have to go into detail because I'm pretty sure you remember the countless bitches that used to confront me back in the day. I'm going to tell you this because I experienced being with a cheating ass nigga before. All I got to say is know your worth. That nigga will only do whatever it is that you're allowing him to do. You let him cheat and don't say shit, he going to keep doing it. I think with me, I was so damn stupidly in love with your brother back then and happy that he had finally made me his girl, that I would let him do anything and accept it. I was a teenager then, who didn't know any better though. You a grown ass woman, Shay, who takes care of yourself, so you don't need that nigga for shit in the first place," I told her and she nodded her head.

"It's just that I love him already, so much, Shonte. And I do have a bad habit of accepting some of the shit that he does because he'll turn around and buy me things and fuck the shit out of me to the point where I just forget what I was arguing about in the first place," she said, making both of us laugh. "No, but seriously, Shonte. I know I'm not supposed to be accepting that, but it's so hard because I feel like I can't let him go that easily. You know I gave this nigga my damn virginity?" La'shay said to me in a harsh whisper.

I remember when we were younger, she would always tell me that she was saving herself for that special someone, now I'm wondering if

Tez's ass had been the special someone for all for all of these damn years. I'm not going to lie, I was a little hurt finding out about La'shay and Tez this way because Shay and I were damn near sisters and we told each other everything. Even though I was a little hurt behind it, I played it off because right now wasn't the time or the place for that conversation.

"You know your brother came home the other night asking me if I knew about you and Tez fuckin' around. I told his ass straight up that I didn't. Girlll, that nigga was so hot in that bedroom that night about his little sister finally dating, and I didn't make the shit any better when I told him that you were probably fuckin' now too," I said, causing the two of us to burst out laughing.

"Now you know you ain't right for telling Jarvis that. Don't feel any type of way either about me not telling you. You already know that certain shit I don't tell your ass because you break when Jarvis asks you things about me and tell him," La'shay said.

I couldn't argue about that because it was the damn truth.

We continued talking while I sat and ate two slices of the cheese pizza that the staff had just brought over to the table. After I finished eating, I got a funny feeling in my stomach and I had the sudden urge to throw up. I shot up so damn fast from that table, like someone had put fire on my ass and rushed to the nearest restroom. As soon as I made it inside, I went into the first stall and threw up all of the pizza that I had just eaten. As I was squatting over the toilet, I heard the door to the restroom open and then close, which was followed by me letting more vomit out of my system.

"Shonte!" I heard Jarvis call my name. Leave it to his ass to come into the women's restroom.

"I'm in here," I said, out of breath as I reached back and unlocked the stall door for him. I had my back to him, but I could feel his eyes burning a hole through me.

"Yeahhh, that's what the fuck I'm talking about!" I heard Jarvis chant from behind me.

I stood up and looked at his ass like he was crazy.

"What the hell are you talking about, Jarvis?" I asked him as I flushed the toilet and walked out of the stall.

As I waited for his response, I washed my hands and rinsed my mouth. I needed to get back to my purse so that I could chew on some gum, or whatever type of mint I had inside. It would just have to do until I made it back home to some mouthwash.

"That was one of the symptoms of pregnancy, throwing up," Jarvis said.

I literally didn't even think pregnancy as I was on my knees puking my guts out. Well, at least that's not what I wanted to think. I waved Jarvis off and then grabbed a paper towel and wiped around my mouth.

"If I was pregnant, Jarvis, trust me I would know," I told him.

I tried to walk away, but he pulled me close to him, putting a strong grip on my ass. He looked down at me with a cocky grin on his face. I'd be lying if I said that his handsome ass wasn't making me wet with the way that he was staring at me. I just could not seem to get enough of this man. Whenever I was around him, I would always get those butterflies in my stomach and feel like that same silly little fifteen-year-old girl again.

"Technically, if you were pregnant, I would be the first to know. The last two times you got pregnant, I didn't know. For the first time, after I slid up in you at the prison, I never got to feel that pussy again. Then, the next time, I wasn't fuckin' with you like that, so I wasn't around to know. This time, I just know. Shonte, I come home from work and fuck you every night raw, and your ass ain't on no type of birth control either. Weren't you complaining yesterday about your breasts being sore? Then, why all of a sudden when a nigga was trying to get balls deep in you last night, you were pushing at my chest, talking about that shit hurt? Most importantly, since when the hell you throw up after eating cheese pizza?" Jarvis asked me, cocking his head to the side.

"You really think you know everything, huh?"

"Nah, but when it comes to you, you damn right I'm claiming to know everything," he told me and then he leaned his head in and placed a kiss on my lips.

I wrapped my arms around his neck and slowly eased my tongue into his mouth. He gladly accepted it. Jarvis picked me up, walked over to the bathroom door and locked it. He placed me on the edge of the sink, and it hit me why he had locked the door.

"Jarvis, no! Just wait until we get home," I told him, but clearly my voice fell on deaf ears because he was now at the button of the too little shorts that I was wearing and he was pulling them down.

"I should just knock your ass out for coming out the house in these tiny ass shorts. Fuck is wrong with you, girl? Got all my shit on full display for all these niggas to see!" Jarvis barked at me with a sexy ass scowl on his face. Clearly, his ass wasn't that mad if he was still trying to get some pussy out of me.

"You mad at me, daddy?" I asked him, unzipping his pants and pulling his dick out through the slit of his boxers.

He was already good and hard for me. I used the head of his dick to rub it in circles across my clit, making my pussy get even wetter. Jarvis had both of his hands behind me, on either side of the wall, and he was allowing me to pleasure myself with his dick.

"Put him in there, baby! Let me feel some of that pregnant pussy," Jarvis said to me in a low, sexy voice.

I eased his dick into my opening and we both let out satisfied moans. "Let me put some more dick in there, baby," Jarvis whispered in my ear and then he stuck his tongue in it, which made chills run down my spine. Just like how I was doing him last night, I was fighting him off of me because I felt that same pain that I felt when he had popped my cherry years ago.

"Ohhhh… Jaarrvisss," I cried out once he was all the way inside of me. He started fucking me with long, slow grinds. It hurt so much that it actually felt good, if that even made sense.

"I'm right here, baby. I ain't going nowhere. See the crazy shit this pussy makes me do? We supposed to be at our son's birthday party, yet I got you in here tucked away because I couldn't wait until we got back home to slide back in this pussy. Shit too good, man! Fuck!" he growled in my ear and he went to attacking my neck.

I couldn't even reply to what he was saying. All I could do was sit there and take that dick, and let these moans continue to escape from my mouth.

"I'm about to cum, babbbyy," I moaned into his ear.

He sped up his pace, and a few seconds later, we both came at the same time. My body shook underneath him as I came down from my orgasmic high. "God, you always know how to make my body feel good," I told him as I placed kisses all along his face.

I always expressed to Jarvis how good he made me feel after we finished having sex because I felt that as a woman, you should let your man know that he is handling his business and keeping you on your toes when it comes to sex. I knew Jarvis really didn't need to hear me say it because his cocky ass knew it already.

I was still seated on top of the sink when Jarvis went over and grabbed some paper towels, wet them, and then cleaned between my legs. Once he was finished, he placed a kiss on my pussy and picked me up, placing me on my feet. We both got dressed and then a few minutes later, we walked out of the bathroom together.

I called this right here the "walk of shame". Let's be real, every adult in the building knew what had just taken place because we had disappeared at least thirty minutes ago. On top of that, instead of the ponytail that I had before, I just pulled all of my hair up into a bun. Plus, the passion marks that were on my neck and chest area, weren't there before I went in.

"Ma, I was looking for you! Your friend who we saw at the mall was here and she gave me this," Javari said, running up on me and handing me a small box. It was light as hell, so I wondered what the hell was inside of it.

"What friend from the mall?" I asked Javari because I had no idea who the hell his ass was even talking about.

"Ma, the lady we saw when you, me, and Auntie Shay was at the mall. I gotta go, me and my friends about to get back on the go-kart," Javari told me and then he took off running.

I kept thinking about who the hell he was talking about, and that's when I remembered that he was with me the day in the mall where I had run into Malaya. I quickly opened the box, and inside were two bullets and a note was attached to each one that read, *One for you, and one for Mommy.*

Jarvis was standing right beside me, so he saw the whole thing. In seconds, the two of us took off, trying to see if this bitch was anywhere lurking in this damn building. The fact that she had gotten so close to my damn son without Jarvis or my knowledge scared the hell out of me. Damn, what if she had taken my baby? Lord knows I would have died if I came back from the bathroom after having sex, only to find that my son was gone.

All of a sudden, I just fuckin' panicked. I hunched my body over and started wheezing. I needed my asthma pump right now, but it was so far away. I fell to the floor trying to catch my breath, and that's when I saw one of the kids from Javari's school walk past me.

"Javari... Javarii... get him," I told him, barely able to get those words out of my mouth.

The little boy took off running, and a few minutes later, Javari came running over to me with my purse, along with majority of my other family members that were in attendance. Javari quickly went through my purse, pulled out my inhaler and passed it to me. I removed the cap, shook the inhaler and tilted my head back, bringing the inhaler to my mouth to release the medicine into me.

When I finished, my mom ran over to me, kissing me on my cheek and wiping away at the beads of sweat that had appeared on my forehead. I'll admit that this experience was enough to scare the shit out of my ass. I was so far away from my inhaler, and I didn't have the energy to walk and get it. Thank God for Javari's friend because it's no telling what the hell would have happened had I not run into him.

"You okay, baby? God, you scared the hell out of me. Almost gave my ass a heart attack," my mom said to me.

I nodded my head, assuring her that I was all right.

After I calmed down, we went back over to the section where Javari's party was being held. At that point, all I wanted to do was go home and lay my ass down. I hated the advantage that Malaya bitch had on me, because she was about to be the reason why my son's party had ended early.

About ten minutes later, Jarvis came back into the room with a pissed off look on his face. I wasn't even going to add more stress to him about my episode. I didn't want to further upset him. We gathered up all of the kids, sang happy birthday to my son, and after another hour or so, we all left. To my surprise, Javari wasn't mad about leaving early because he had summed it up to me not feeling well, and he was okay with that.

*Later that night*

"Shonte, I need you to trust me and know that I would never allow anybody to hurt you or my damn son. That's my fuckin' word, man. When you left me back then after that shit that Mya and her home girls did to you, that was a fuckin' wake up call for my ass. The feeling of being without your significant other is a fucked up feeling, and I would never want to feel that way again, yo! You and my son are the two most important people in my life, so just know that y'all good," Jarvis told me, placing a kiss on my forehead.

We were in bed lying down, and I'm guessing he could tell by how quiet I had been since we made it home that I was still feeling some type of way about Malaya being that close to my son.

That night when Jarvis and I rode back to the park and saw that her car wasn't there anymore, I knew then that the bitch wasn't dead, but how the hell she knew that we would be at Extreme Action Park today was crazy to me. I'm just thankful that Javari wasn't the one who had opened the gift.

"Can you promise me something, Jarvis?" I asked him.

He was sitting up in the bed smoking, while I had my head resting on his chest. This was something that had been on my mind for a while now.

"What is it?"

I needed to look him in his eyes when I asked him this, so I pushed the covers away from my body and straddled his lap. I looked him dead in the eyes when I talked to him and he did the same thing for me. "Promise me that if you catch her before I do that you won't kill her. I want to be the one to do it. Never in my life have I felt so strongly about wanting a person dead as much as I want Malaya dead. That woman killed our baby, and I don't like the fact that she was so close to Javari, so please promise me this," I told him.

Jarvis took a long pull from his joint and then he looked me square in the eyes.

"I promise," he told me, sealing the deal with a kiss to my lips.

After he made that promise to me, I climbed out of his lap and got back on my side of the bed. Now I knew what 2pac meant when he quoted, "I ain't a killer but don't push me!". Clearly, I had been pushed, and the bullets that she had stamped with my son's and my name on it were going to be the same two bullets that would kill her ass once and for all.

# CHAPTER 12

## *Malaya Brown*

Shonte realllyyy needed to be careful of the shit that she posted on social media, because thanks to her, I was able to find out that she would be celebrating her son's fifth birthday at Extreme Action Park yesterday. If you asked me, the bitch was just making this shit way too easy for me because I didn't even plan on fuckin' with her today, but I decided, why not? Besides, I wanted this bitch to know that I was very much alive and kicking. Dumb bitch really thought that she had taken me out for good with that little choke she had given me that day at the park. She would find out sooner or later that I was a damn good actress, so it was nothing for me to roll my eyes in the back of my head and hold my breath, letting the bitch think that she had killed me off.

I swear I wanted to burst out laughing when I watched her scary ass run off to her car and pull out of the parking lot. I'll admit that the bitch had hands and could fight her ass off. That night, she tore my ass up in that parking lot, and I had never lost a fight until then.

Anyway, today I had pulled up to the park where the party was, but I was in full disguise. I was dressed in all black and wearing a hat and some dark ass sunglasses because I couldn't blow my cover. I knew for a fact that if Jarvis or Shonte had caught me in here, they would make no mistake about killing my ass in broad daylight, in the middle of all of those people.

I happened to be standing over by the go-karts when I noticed Jarvis and Shonte's handsome baby boy. Most women would have kidnapped his lil cute ass if they had this obsession like I did, but honestly I didn't want him. I wanted to be the one to give Jarvis new babies. On top of that, I didn't want anything that would be of a reminder of Shonte's ass, so her and her son had to go.

"Javari," I had called out his name.

He looked at me strangely and then ignored me, focusing on being the next person in the line to get on the go-kart. Since that wouldn't make him come, I decided to pull out the gift box that I had in my purse and I showed it to him. That got his attention because a few seconds later, he was coming in my direction. I took the glasses off my face once he was close enough.

"You remember me, don't you?" I asked him.

He looked at me for a while and then it hit him. "Oh yeah, You're my mommy's friend from the mall," he told me.

"That's right. Here, happy birthday little man! Give this to Mommy when you see her," I said, handing him the box and getting the fuck out of dodge because right when I handed it to him, he took off running to find his mother, so that he could give her the gift.

I knew once Shonte opened the box and found what was inside, she would be scanning the room, searching for my ass. I made it to my car within two minutes and waited because I knew sooner or later, her or Jarvis were going to come outside looking to see if I was in the parking lot. Sure enough, about five minutes later, I watched as Jarvis' eyes scanned through the parking lot. I almost came on myself just by looking at all of that sexiness. I swear, he was sexier when he was pissed the fuck off and stressed. I pulled my phone out of my pocket and snapped pictures of him because I was tired of the same ones that I had hanging up of him in my bedroom. After he didn't find what he was looking for, he took his ass back into the building and I pulled out of the parking lot.

That was yesterday. Now today, I had a few other things up my sleeve. I wanted to pay Shonte's precious parents a little visit. I knew for a fact that Shonte wouldn't be over there because I had just finished stalking her Facebook page and she was telling her business as usual on how Jarvis had paid for her a full day at the spa. I swear, that bitch irked my damn nerves, man! The thing about it, Shonte had already hit her 5,000 mark on the number of friends that she could have, and I assumed that was the reason why she had made her page public. It was beneficial to me because I was able to know whether I could act on a move or not.

Right now, I was pulling up in the driveway of Shonte's parent's house, and there was only one car in the driveway. The last time I had followed her there, it was two cars in the driveway, so I assumed that someone probably wasn't home. I turned the car off and then got out. After knocking on the door, I waited for someone to answer. I knocked for a good five minutes and no one came to the door. *Hmmm, I guess I'll just come back another time.*

After getting back into my car, I made my way back to my mother's house. When I pulled up, there was a police car parked in the driveway. I immediately began to panic, but I didn't want to turn back around because then I'd look suspicious. If this was a detective, I'm pretty sure this wasn't his first time seeing the house. The officer had probably seen this car parked in the driveway a few times, so I couldn't just turn around now.

I pulled the car in behind him, parked and got out. One of my specialties is acting, so I was about to put on my best performance with whoever was sitting in that car waiting for me. I may have been able to fool other people with my crocodile tears, but if that was a fuckin' detective in that car, them niggas specialized in body language and probably had taken a few psychology courses, so they would know if I was bullshitting them or not.

"Hey, I'm Detective Tony. You are?" he asked me, stepping out of his car as another detective got out of the passenger seat.

I'm not going to lie, Detective Tony was fine as hell, and I couldn't help to stare at him in awe. He stood about 6'3" and he had the body of a NFL player, with all of the muscles and shit that he had going on. Tony was the type of fine that you had to question whether or not he was straight. I mean, this nigga's eyebrows were almost shaped better than mine was. I observed everything from his fingernails, which didn't have any dirt in them, his perfect white teeth, all the way down to the print of his dick in the slacks that he was wearing. Tony's skin complexion looked almost as if it was kissed by the sun, and he was clearly in competition with the ocean by the waves that he had in his hair. With all of that said, I would never get the chance to fuck with him on that level because Lord knows I didn't fuck with the law.

"Malaya Brown," I told him.

I had to play it cool. I didn't want them thinking that I was up to anything at all. I'm not stupid though, so I knew exactly why they were there in the first place.

"Hmmm, Malaya Brown. Why does that name sound so familiar?" his partner asked.

I could tell that he was trying to be sarcastic, but I didn't pay his ass any attention. His partner was nowhere near as fine as Tony was. In fact, his partner could use a few laps around the track and some proactive for the acne that he had on his face.

"That's my partner, Detective Davis," Tony said, pointing toward his partner. I just nodded my head. "You mind coming down to the station for questioning? We just have a few things that we need to go over with you."

"In regards to what?" I asked.

"Teresa Brown. Does that name ring any bells?"

"Of course it does. That's my mother. Is everything alright with her?" I asked, making my voice crack as I spoke, and causing my eyes to get watery. *This shit was way too easy!*

"That's what we're trying to figure out. We won't keep you long. Like I said, we just need a few questions answered," Tony told me and I nodded my head.

I followed them to the police car and I sat in the back. The drive to the precinct was enough time for me to get my lies and loose ends in order because I already knew that they were about to start questioning the hell out of my ass, trying to get me to confess to some shit that they didn't have any proof that I had done. They would just be going off assumptions and trying to get me to tell on myself. I had cleaned up my tracks well with all four murders that I had committed, so nothing should trace back to me.

We finally pulled up to the precinct and I was placed in a cold room, where I couldn't see out the glass. I had watched enough first 48 to know that it was muthafuckas behind that glass watching my body language. *Don't twiddle your thumbs because you'll look guilty. Try to keep still because you'll look nervous if you keep moving around. Let a few tears fall, so you'll look distraught.* I coached myself the entire time that I sat there, and then a few minutes later the detectives came into the room, both of them carrying a pen and pad in their hands.

"You okay, Ms. Brown? You need a water or anything?" Detective Tony asked me.

"No, I'm fine. I would just like to know what's going on with my mother," I stated, causing Davis to chuckle.

I could already see that his ass was going to be a problem, with his fat ass. Tony was okay because he was at least trying to make me feel comfortable, and his eyes weren't as accusing as Davis' were.

"Okay, I'm going to get straight to the point. When is the last time you saw your mother?" Tony asked me.

Well, technically, the last time I saw her was when I killed her ass, but clearly I couldn't tell them that.

"It had to be a few months ago when she and I were in the living room watching TV together," I said.

"Wait, hold on. So, you're agreeing that the last time you saw your mom was a few months ago? Ms. Brown, is that the norm for you to go that long without being in communication with your mother?" Detective Tony asked me after he finished writing something down.

"You see, that's where you're wrong! I never said that I stopped being in communication with my mom a few months ago. I agreed to not having seen her in a few months. Yes, that is the norm for my mother and I because she has a boyfriend who occupies most of her time, which leaves me to have the house to myself a lot," I explained.

"I see, and your mother's boyfriend, what's he's like? What's his name?" this time Davis asked the questions.

"My mother's boyfriend's name is Deon. He's a good guy, I'm assuming. I don't really know him like that because I only met him a handful of times. I mean, he couldn't be that bad if my mother was spending all of her time with him," I said, letting out a sarcastic laugh.

"I'm going to cut right to the chase, Ms. Brown. We have strong reason to believe that your mother, Teresa Brown, could be dead or missing. We received a call the other day from her job claiming that your mother hadn't been to work in two months. They said she hasn't called or anything, and that behavior like that wasn't normal for her because she had been working there for over ten years and she has never missed a day of work. Fast forward two days later, we get a call from the church that she attends, letting us know the same thing. They say that Ms. Brown attends church faithfully, and that when they come over to the house, no one opens the door. Now, I'm going to ask you again, when is the last time that you had contact with your mother?" Detective Brown asked me. This time, he was a little bit more stern with his approach.

"I told you, the last time that I saw my mother was a few months ago, but I talked to her maybe sometime last week. Just because I don't have the ideal mother and daughter relationship and I don't see my mother quite as often as I would like, why should that determine me being guilty in any of this?" I asked.

"And what exactly is any of this, Ms. Brown? Do you know something that we don't know? You know the law. You look like a smart girl, so we clearly cannot say you're guilty until we prove it," Detective Davis' smart ass went on to say.

"You didn't have to say it, but your questions are speaking volumes right now! The first time I said that I hadn't seen my mother in a few months, why wasn't that enough? Why did you have to go and ask me that again like I would just change my answer or some shit?" I wanted to know.

"Ms. Brown, please calm down. No one is trying to accuse you of anything. We would just like some questions answered," Detective Tony intervened.

"Listen, at the end of the day, my mother and I haven't had a close bond in years. Her not coming to the house and seeing me to check up on me is normal to me. I'm actually used to people putting things and people before me. A few hours ago when you saw me get out of that car, I was about to walk into an empty home. I have no one. A few months ago, I lost my only sister, hell, the only friend that I ever had, and my nephew as well. Now, you're coming and telling me that you think my mother is dead! How many more fuckin' deaths in the family can I take before I just fuckin' break?" I banged my hand on the table as tears fell from my eyes.

*Come through, sis!* I coached myself because I was carrying on better than Taraji P. Henson when her ass gets to crying in a movie. The sad part about it, I wasn't getting paid to do this shit.

"Ms. Brown, I'm so sorry about the death of your sister and your nephew, I really am! We're not claiming death on your mother yet, but it is a strong possibility. What about friends? Does your mom have people that she is close with? Even enemies? Anybody out there who would want to bring harm to your mother?" Detective Tony asked me.

He was so sincere, and I could tell that he really wanted to get down to the nitty gritty in the disappearance of my mother.

"My mom didn't really have friends like that. Just a few associates from work or from the church. She didn't really have any enemies either because my mom was a nice person and would give her right arm to a stranger if she had to."

That part right there wasn't me acting, it was honestly the truth. My mother was really a sweet person, but I felt like I had kind of changed her in a way with the first murder that I committed when I was only fifteen years old. I felt like she was in a constant battle with herself when I came back to live with her because she just didn't act the same. The beautiful smile that she used to wear on her chocolate face would sort of look back at me with eyes of resentment. I often wondered if it was hate as well, but I never could tell.

There was a five-minute pause because both detectives were writing down notes. As they were writing, I was pretty much saving all the information that I had just confessed to in my subconscious because I wasn't stupid. I knew they were going to try and hit me with the same questions later on down the line to see if I would switch my story up. Many people don't know this, but that's how a lot of criminals are caught, because they didn't know how to keep a lie going. Me, on the other hand, I was a natural born liar and a con artist, so I felt like I didn't have anything to really worry about.

"Detectives, if that's it, do you mind if I go now? I've been up since early this morning, and I would like to just go home and lie down," I asked them, faking a yawn as I talked.

"Sure, you can go ahead and leave, Ms. Brown. If there's anything else we need from you, trust me, we know how to find you. In the meantime, take my card, and if you happen to hear from your mom or anything, please give us a call," Detective Tony said, standing up and handing me his card, which had his personal cell on it and his work phone number.

I took the card from him and placed it in my wallet. Nodding my head, I let him know that I would definitely give him a phone call if something were to come up, even though I knew that was the furthest thing from the truth.

"Oh wait, I just thought about it. You rode with us here, so we have to take you back home," Detective Tony said.

I had forgotten that I had rode with them as well. I had been in this room with them for what felt like forever, and I had completely forgotten that I didn't drive my own car.

"You know what, it's fine. With everything that I just found out, I can actually use the walk to clear my head," I told him.

I really just didn't want to get back in the car with them because I wasn't up for another interrogation, which is what I knew they were going to do.

"Are you sure? It's no problem for us to take you back home," Tony said.

"Seriously, I'll be fine," I reassured him.

"I'll walk you out then," Detective Davis jumped in.

I looked at his ass like he was crazy, but I didn't say anything. I just walked over to the door and turned the handle.

When we made it into the hallway, there was an awkward silence between the two of us. I led the way, while he trailed along in the back. As soon as we got outside, I stood by the stairs and Davis jumped right in front of me.

"Listen to me Malaya, and listen to me good. I know for a fact that you killed your mother, your sister, and your nephew. I even know about the way you man slaughtered Mr. Ronald Jones, a.k.a Tank! You got away that time, but I put this on my life that I won't let you walk away that easy. If it's the last thing that I do, I'm going to make sure that you never see the light of day ever again," Davis told me with so much malice dropping off of each word that he spoke.

His words didn't move me because at the end of the day, I wasn't sloppy with my shit, so therefore, he would never be able to prove that I had anything to do with the death of my mother, Mya, Justin, or Deon.

"Have a good day, Detective," I told him and then turned on my heels to leave.

# CHAPTER 13

## Detective Tony

*I* wasn't some donut eating muthafucka who came to work every day just wanting to fuck with innocent bystanders or some shit like that. With all of the craziness going on in the world, you had to actually be careful with the way you handled certain situations, or should I say certain people. You see, I wasn't like most detectives, in fact, my partner Davis and I were like night and day. If Davis brought in a possible suspect, he would do everything in his power to make that person feel uncomfortable, and it wouldn't be a secret that he thinks that they are guilty. Myself, on the other hand, I liked to play it smooth. I wanted my possible suspect to be as comfortable as possible when they're in my presence, because then they would think that I'm on their team, and maybe, just maybe, they can get away with the crime that they could have possibly committed.

I was playing the hell out of Malaya Brown, the same way she was playing the hell out of me with those crocodile tears that she had flowing down her face. I had put in over twenty years in my career, so I could smell bullshit from a mile away, and Malaya had bullshit right up her fuckin' alley! I would never understand how someone so beautiful could do shit that was so hateful.

I sat there in the interrogation room that Malaya had just walked out of and looked over the areas where I had placed question marks. Whenever I would place a question mark by a note, often times it meant that something the suspect told me just wasn't adding up. I sat there for a few more minutes and then the door opened. I turned around and it was Davis walking in with this silly smirk on his face.

"Come on, Tony! What you thinking? I know for a fact that she did this shit, why aren't you seeing what I'm seeing?" Davis asked me, closing the door behind him and then taking a seat in front of me. Davis was always so ready to jump the gun, and often times we would butt heads, but he had been my partner for years, so we kind of leveled each other out.

"Davis, calm down! I never said that I don't see what you're seeing! I know that Ms. Brown is responsible for those murders, but you've been in business long enough to know that we can't go to the D.A. off of what we feel or what we believe in the court house! We need fuckin' evidence, man! We need shit that will stick! Trust me, man, I want to see her behind bars for the rest of her life just like you, but in due time, my man! In due fuckin' time!" I told Davis.

He just sat there and shook his head. I ran my hands through my hair and looked at him for a few seconds. "You want to know how I know that she's guilty?" I asked Davis.

He looked at me with a question in his eyes, so I went ahead and told him.

"It's like that was it. After she did all of her crying about her mother when I told her that there was a possibility of her being dead, that was it! She never asked any more questions. She just didn't come off as a person who had just found out about her mother being missing for the first time. It was almost as if she knew this piece of information already, but she had to act as if it was new to her. I've dealt with hundreds of cases, and to come to someone and tell them that a family member, not just any family member but a mother could possibly be dead, you don't just cry for two minutes and then be okay, and you damn sure cannot be in your right state of mind to be able to walk the ten blocks to get back to your house! Also, notice how quick she was to say that we were accusing her of something? Only a person who's guilty would react that way, because clearly they have something to hide. With all of that, Davis, we cannot hold this in a courtroom. But trust me man, we won't let her get off easy this time," I told him.

Davis let what I said marinate for a little bit, and then he stood up from his seat and gave me a pound. At that moment, I knew that him and I were definitely on the same page. After staying behind at the office for a few more hours, I was finally in my car own my way home. Don't get me wrong, I loved my job, but I'll be damned if the shit wasn't tiring. Lucky for me, I had someone to come home to at night and relieve all of my stress. The someone that I had at home waiting for me, we had been kicking it for a few months now, but we've just made our relationship official. I couldn't wait to get home.

About thirty minutes later, I pulled up at the condo that I lived in out in Miramar. I parked, grabbed my briefcase, and I was out the car. I took the stairs, which led me to the third floor and I let myself in.

Immediately, the smell of spaghetti filled my nose, causing a smile to form on my face because Lord knows I was starving.

"Baby, where you at?" I called, setting my briefcase by the door and then going to find my lover.

"I'm in here," the deep, masculine voice called back, and I made my way to the kitchen.

Standing before me was my lover in only a pair of navy blue Calvin Klein boxers. I walked up behind him and wrapped my arms around his waist as he stood in front of the stove, moving the spoon around in the food. I kissed him on his neck and watched as his body shuddered against mine.

"How was your day, baby?" he asked me, turning around and wrapping his arms around my neck.

"You already know how that goes. But what about you? How was your day? You standing in front of me in nothing but your draws, so I'm assuming that you must have tied up those loose ends that you've been telling me about," I said and then brought my head in closer so that I could kiss him on his full lips.

"Not yet, but baby, I promise that it's going to happen soon. Come on now, cut a nigga some slack. I'm not even sleeping in the same bed with her or no shit like that. Only reason why I'm still over there is because I want to be closer to my baby," he told me.

Immediately, I was irritated, so I pushed him away from me and stared at him with a pissed off look on my face.

"Chad, how much fuckin' longer are you going to say this shit to me? You've been saying for the past few months that you were done with your baby mama, but I honestly can't tell because you haven't left the bitch yet! I have no problem with you being a man and being there for your child, but I don't feel like you should have to sleep there in order for you to accomplish that! If you're asleep and the baby is asleep at night, why should you have to sleep there? I've been holding my tongue on this for a while now because I didn't want to start any drama, but you and I aren't just friends with benefits anymore! We fuck, and you tell me that you love me on a daily. On top of that, you're my fuckin' boyfriend, Chad! What's so hard about you moving in with me?" I asked him. God, I just wanted to know because this was ridiculous.

I got no response from him, so I just shook my head. "Oh, I get it! You're ashamed, right? You're embarrassed for your friends and family to know that you like sucking dick and taking it up the ass, right? Listen here, I've been considered to be your homeboy long enough, so I deserve better. Not once have I ever asked you to be here with me, so if our relationship is too much for you, you can leave, Chad! I refuse to be your secret lover anymore!" I yelled at him.

For months, when Chad and I would go out, we would always just tell people that we were homeboys, but behind closed doors, we were actually fucking the shit out of each other. I wanted more now. I've changed a lot of my ways for him, and he couldn't even change this one thing for me, which was to come out to his family and move in with me. He made it seem like it was the hardest fuckin' thing in the world to do.

At the end of the day, family is supposed to love you no matter what, so if his family stopped loving him because of the way that he chooses to live his life, then clearly he doesn't need them in his corner. Now, his baby mama on the other hand, I already knew that she wasn't going to be so accepting about his revelation. I mean, what woman would?

Before Chad and I established this bond that we have, we were friends and he opened up to me about his sexuality and how he would often catch himself staring at men. The man even told me that he's never in his life given a woman oral sex. Right then and there, I knew his ass was gay, which was all right with me because it was something about Chad that I just couldn't resist. It took a lot of courage for him to tell me these things, and I felt honored that I was the first person who he had gone to with this this piece of information.

Me, on the other hand, I had been gay for as long as I could remember, and I wasn't ashamed to admit it either. At a young age, I knew for a fact that I didn't want to be playing any type of manly sports, but I wouldn't mind sticking around to watch the sexy ass boys play, though. At the end of the day, I could see where Chad was coming from about being afraid to come out to his parents because my own dam daddy stopped fuckin' with me once I officially came out of the closet. I wasn't about to force somebody to love me or no shit like that just because they didn't agree with my lifestyle. I also wasn't about to keep trying to hold onto a man who clearly wasn't ready to be kept.

"Chad, I love you, but I love me more. So, with that being said, if you can't come to some type of resolution by the end of the month, then I love you enough to let you go."

I kissed his lips and then turned to take the stairs and go on up to my room. I needed him to let the words that I had just spoken to him marinate because Lord knows that I was telling the truth this time. It wouldn't be any more chances after this one.

# CHAPTER 14

## Shonte Howard

Right now, Jarvis and I were at his mother's house, after just coming back from the doctor's office to find out that I was four weeks pregnant. I swear it was a damn shame that Jarvis knew my damn body better than I did. I mean, this man knew right off the bat that I was pregnant once he caught me throwing up in the stall a few weeks ago at our son's birthday party. This pregnancy, I already knew that I had to be very careful because Lord knows that I couldn't have another episode of what happened to me in my last pregnancy. I swear, I still have nightmares about that damn dog and falling down those stairs. I often find myself thinking about that day, just thinking about what the hell would have happened if I had Javari with me that day.

Anyway, on a more positive note, this pregnancy right here is super special. Jarvis was incarcerated during my first pregnancy, and my second one, Jarvis wasn't really fuckin' with me like that, but he was still going to doctor appointments with me. For as long as Jarvis and I have been together, I feel like this is the first time ever that we are actually getting it right. I mean, this Jarvis Banks right here even allows me to pick up his phone when it rings and even go through his shit. The old Jarvis Banks would have killed my ass dead if I even looked as if I was going to answer his phone. I guess what I'm trying to say is that I'm very appreciative of the faithful man that I have now.

Bitches think that shit is cute when a man cheats and you continue to take him back because he drops you off some dick and money, but honestly, as women, we have to learn to stop being so weak and put our foot down. Show these niggas that we're worth more than that, and that he isn't the only man in this world that we could have. That's pretty much what I had to do with Jarvis. It fucked his pride up badly to see me with Chad and to even be engaged to him. Niggas will make you swear to them that you would never give their pussy away, so the fact that I had given another man what Jarvis had been claiming for years, just didn't sit well with him.

"Well, damn, son! Now, all you got to do is chew the shit up and feed it to her," Jarvis's mother, Regina said to Jarvis, causing me to burst out laughing.

We were sitting at the island in her kitchen, and Jarvis was feeding me soup.

"Ma, quit hating on a nigga," Jarvis told his mother, putting another spoon filled with noodles and broth into my mouth.

"I never could stand the two of y'all anyways," she said, laughing.

I knew what she was referring to because in our younger days, I didn't care if Regina was around, I would still be all over her son. I just loved him that much, so I always made sure to show him. I found myself laughing out loud because I remember when I was eighteen years old and I had spent the night. Regina walked in on Jarvis and I having sex in the bathroom. I swear, I have never been so embarrassed in my damn life.

"I already know what you laughing at over there. You better be lucky I didn't tell your mama on your ass that day!" Regina told me.

"What she was going to do to me, Ma? She already knew Jarvis and I were having sex. She knew the first time, talking about my *walk was different*," I said, mocking the bullshit that my mom had told me years ago, when she just magically knew that I wasn't a virgin anymore. Surprisingly, she wasn't even mad at me, she just wanted me to practice safe sex because I was only in high school at the time, and me popping up pregnant wasn't an option for her.

We continued talking, and then a few minutes later, the front door opened and we all watched as La'shay walked into the house with an annoyed look on her beautiful face. La'shay was dressed casually in a pair of yoga tights from Victoria secret that had the big print VS on the side of them, with the matching sports bra. Her long hair was pulled up into a ponytail, with a big Nike hat on her head and some Pink Roshe Runs on her feet. The hickies that she had on her neck were fairly noticeable, and I already knew that Jarvis felt some type of way because his jaws clenched.

I shook my head because this damn boy could not take the fact that his sister was fuckin' Devontez lightly. I said "fuckin" because La'shay wouldn't tell me if they were really in a relationship or not.

She walked into the kitchen, kissed her mom on the cheek and then looked at me. "Shonte, ride with me right quick."

I could tell from the look in her eyes that she was on some good bullshit. I, already knew what she wanted because the shit was written all over her face. Too many times I had come to her back in the days for her to ride with me to do a pop up on her brother, so I couldn't just turn her down right now because she had always taken that ride with me, no matter the time of day.

"So, I guess you don't see a nigga sitting here?" Jarvis spoke up.

"Jarvis, please, not right now," La'shay told him.

"Fuck you mean 'not right now'? What the fuck is wrong with you, girl? If that nigga fuckin' up, it ain't nothing but a word, and I'll go talk to his ass! You my little sister, La'shay, and I ain't about to have no nigga out here dogging your ass," Jarvis said.

I loved the way he was so overprotective of La'shay. When their dad died, he had to step up, and he did a damn good job when it came to looking after his sister, even if at times he did go a little bit too far with the whole big brother role.

"Jarvis, I got it!" she said, coming over and wrapping her arms around him and then kissing his cheek as well. "Shonte, you coming or what?" she asked me.

"Baby, I'll meet you at the house. Are you going to pick Javari up from my parents or do you want me to do it?" I asked him, standing up from my seat.

"Go ahead, I'll get him when I leave. Shonte, you pregnant, so don't go out there doing some shit that's gon' get you fucked up!" he said, pulling me in by my waist and kissing me on my lips.

"I'm not. I love you" I said, backing away from him.

"I love you more," he told me.

"Bye, Ma," I said to Regina and kissed her cheek before I left.

La'shay had already gone outside and was waiting for me to get in the car. When I got in, she had her GPS going and I wondered where the hell she was about to take us. I fastened my seatbelt and she took off like a bat out of hell.

"I swear I'm going to fuck around and kill this nigga, Shonte! I love him so much, but damn, how much can a bitch take before I fuckin' snap? Tell me why I just called his ass a few minutes ago after I left the gym and he had a bitch answer his damn phone! Only time that nigga leave his phone unattended is when he's asleep, and I swear to God if he's somewhere laid up with the next bitch, I'm fuckin' both of them up! This is the fuckin' reason right here why I'm not telling people about us because clearly this nigga doesn't take me serious! Fuck, man!" Shay said, hitting the steering wheel.

I don't think I have ever seen my best friend this mad in my entire life, and we had been friends ever since high school. I swear, love was a good thing, but it could actually be a fucked up thing if it wasn't taken serious.

"La'shay, calm the fuck down before you kill both of us in this damn car!" I told her because she was driving reckless, trying to get to Tez's ass. "If you this mad with that nigga, why the fuck didn't you tell Jarvis when he asked you, because you know for a fact he would have handled it for you?" I asked her.

"Because I'm not trying to hear a bunch of 'I told you so's.' Jarvis told me like a week ago how Tez was still out here hoeing around, and that I was going to fuck around and get hurt. Besides, I'm grown, Shonte, and I don't need to be running to Jarvis every time some shit happens. That's the reason he still babies my ass now! Another reason why I'm not going to tell Jarvis and you're not either is because Tez and Jarvis are best friends, and I don't want our beef to get in the middle of their friendship!" La'shay told me.

I just nodded my head because Shay was so fuckin' bullheaded, so no matter what I said, she wasn't going to agree with me.

"How you even know where he's at anyway?" I asked her, since she had a destination in her GPS.

"I downloaded an app on his phone, so I'll know his every move," she said with a sinister smile on her face.

"Bitch, the dick better be good for you to be doing all of this. Only a nigga with some good dick will have a bitch doing pop ups and downloading apps and shit," I told her, causing the two of us to laugh.

"The dick is better than good, it's fuckin' Tony the Tiger Greeeaaattt!" she said, making me cry real life tears at the foolishness that came out of her mouth. "Seriously, though, Shonte, even if he's the only man I've ever been with, so I don't have anyone to compare to him, I already know that he will be the best that I've ever had. I mean, that nigga puts it down in the bedroom. I think that's the reason why I'm tripping now because he just came over and fucked me silly last night, and then left out early this morning, claiming he had to go check on his restaurants."

About two minutes later, we pulled up to some projects out in Allapattah.

"Who the hell he knows that stay in Allapattah?" I asked La'shay.

"This where he from, so he's over here a lot. But honestly, I think he got a lil bitch over here or something because his ass always over here, and then I told you that a bitch answered his phone earlier," La'shay told me, whipping the car in the middle of the parking lot.

This bitch was driving like this wasn't her first time popping up on his ass over here.

"Look, right over there to your right," she told me.

I turned my head and looked, and sure enough, Devontez was posted up on the wall with a whole bunch of niggas. Of course, it was a few birds lurking as well. This nigga Tez was in the projects in a damn Armani suit, chilling like it was nothing. I could see where all of Shay's frustration was coming from because that nigga was just too damn fine to leave him surrounded by so many bitches that were wearing damn near nothing.

"I ain't getting out, Shay. Do what you got to do, and I'll wait in the car," I told her.

I already knew she was about to go over there on some crazy shit, which is why I opted to stay in the car. I wasn't even worried about the women that were standing over there doing anything to La'shay because I already knew that Tez wouldn't let anything happen to her.

"Alright, I won't be gone long. Lock the door," La'shay told me and then she got out.

I watched her as she walked over there, and I shook my head because nothing good was about to come from this situation. I hated that the first serious relationship that La'shay got into had to be like this. Some of the shit that Tez did reminded me so much of the shit that Jarvis used to do to me, and it took years for him to turn into the faithful man that I wanted him to be. I just hoped that La'shay didn't have to go through half of the shit that I had endured, just to be with the one she loved.

# CHAPTER 15

## Devontez Aziel

*I* had been on the block kicking it my niggas that I had grown up with, but I couldn't fucking focus because La'shay had been blowing a nigga up for the past two hours. I already knew she was pissed because of the bitch that answered my phone, but she literally had nothing to worry about because I had already handled that situation. A bitch named Queenie that I used to fuck with before Shay and I got serious was who answered my phone today. Apparently, the bitch was feeling a little bold because her ugly ass home girls were around, so when my phone rang in my hand, she quickly answered it before I even had the chance to react.

I wasn't the type of nigga to go around putting my hands on women because I wouldn't want another nigga putting their hands on my mama or no shit like that. But Queenie struck a fucking nerve by touching my shit, so I had to slap the shit out of her ass for that. Only bitch that I was letting touch my damn phone was Shay because her ass had earned that right when I gave her my fucking heart!

La'shay may not know it, but I loved her ass more than I loved my own mother, and that's crazy because she was the one who birthed me. It was because of my mother and my father that I didn't really know how to love. Growing up with no type of guidance, or no love, a nigga pretty much raised my damn self. All I really had was my brothers, Farrell and Khyree, but that was cut short when Khyree was taken from me two years ago. The shit still felt like it happened yesterday.

Some of the fucked up shit that I was doing to La'shay, trust me, I wasn't doing that shit on purpose. But, damn, a nigga is new to all of this relationship shit. La'shay was trying to change me, and I honestly didn't know if I liked that or not. I mean, that woman was expecting a lot of shit out of nigga, and I was doing it because I loved her, and I didn't want to fuck up so bad to the point where she officially throws the towel on with my ass and moves on.

La'shay threatens me all the time that she's going to find her somebody else to treat her better than me, and even though I always wave that shit off, Lord knows that's the scariest feeling in the world. To even think about my woman being with the next nigga makes my blood boil.

What was so special about La'shay and I was the fact that she wasn't somebody who I just randomly started fucking. I had known Shay damn near her whole life, but I knew that if I were to tell Jarvis that I was feeling his sister, he probably would have killed my ass. Shit was different now because we were both grown, so Jarvis couldn't dictate her life. And I'll be damned if another nigga tells my bitch what to do; brother or not. But Jarvis wasn't that type of brother, though. He didn't try to run La'shay's life, but he damn sure would voice his opinion if he wasn't feeling a move that she was making.

Jarvis had no room to speak up on the way I handled Shay because he would be one hypocrite ass nigga. I had watched firsthand the way he used to dog the shit out of Shonte back in the days. I mean, this nigga would have me covering for his ass so that he could do his little dirt behind her back and shit. I was really trying to get my shit together, and it wasn't to impress Jarvis or no shit like that, but it was for my sake.

I couldn't lose Shay because she's the only female that ever loved my ass. Back in the day, her ass would stare at me with these googly eyes, and that was when a nigga didn't have shit. I dressed dirty looking going to school and all of that, but she would still stare at me like I was Denzel Washington or some shit. That alone was the reason why I spoiled the shit out of her because I knew that she was with me out of pure love, not because of the shit that a nigga had.

"Tez, ain't that your girl walking up?" my brother Farrell asked me, looking up from the dice game that he was playing.

I looked up, and sure enough that was Shay's ass approaching. From the look on her face, I already knew she was about to be on some bullshit. I don't know why, but something about her rolling up on my ass in the hood was sexy as fuck to me, and it kind of made my dick hard. I don't know about these other niggas, but I was the type of nigga who loved to see my girl snapping on my ass. It was something so sexy about all of that eye and neck rolling that just turned a nigga on. It kind of made the love that she had for me more visible because the louder her voice would get or the harder she would roll them damn eyes proved to a nigga that she cared.

I'll admit, though. I had turned the fuck out of Shay these past few months that I've been with her. I remember she used to be so innocent and would barely curse, now her ass was too hyped and ready to lay hands on a nigga every chance she got.

"Where is the bitch that answered your phone, Tez?" she asked me the moment she got close to me.

I could smell her Prada Candy perfume before anything, and that was my favorite scent on her. I admired La'shay in the little outfit that she had on, and I couldn't help but to notice the little gap that she had between her legs ever since she started fucking me. I knew I had the baddest bitch in the whole damn city, so why did I do some of the fucked up shit to her? I have no idea.

"What bitch, Shay?" I asked, pulling her close to me and resting my hands on her ass.

At his point, I could feel all eyes on us. Nobody was used to me being this affectionate with a female, so for me to be all over Shay like this in broad daylight, I already knew the two of us were about to be the talk of the damn town. Nobody really knew Shay and I were dating like that because she wanted to keep it one big secret, but clearly our secret was out now by the way that I was putting on out here.

"You know what bitch I'm talking about, Devontez! Why you do you do shit like this to me? Nobody is forcing you to be with me, nigga, so if being faithful is too much for you, then you're welcome to leave at any time! You know how many niggas are lined up to get at me?" she asked me.

She knew that bullshit would piss me off, so I honestly had no idea why she even said it.

"Just know when them niggas get sent to an early grave, it's going to be because of your ass!" I told her.

It wasn't a threat either, it was a fucking promise. I know I fuck up in more ways than one, but I swear to God that I will kill a nigga for even stepping up to my bitch.

"Why you protecting that hoe, Tez? Tell me where the bitch at that answered your phone! Clearly you care about her since you trying to protect her from me beating her ass!" La'shay said, causing me to laugh because this girl was fuckin' crazy.

"If it makes you feel any better, I slapped the shit out of her ass for touching my shit, and she been gone for about an hour now. What a nigga got to do to prove to your ass that all I want is you? Look at them bitches over there for a minute," I told her, and she looked at the bitches that were on the other side of the building.

They were all staring at Shay with these evil looks on their faces. I'm not even going to lie, I had probably fucked about half of the women that were posted up on that wall, but that wasn't the point that I was trying to make. After she finished looking, I cuffed her chin and then made her look me directly in my eyes.

"Them bitches can't do half the shit that you do for me. I love you! You are who I want to be with, and the sooner you get that through your thick ass head, the better off we'll be!" I told her.

I pulled her close into me, while I let my hands rest on her ass. "I'm about to head out, Tez," she told me, and I could tell that she was feeling some type of way.

"Who you got in the car with you?" I could see a figure in the car moving around, but from where I was standing I couldn't see who it was because I had the tints dark as hell on her car.

"Shonte is in there," she told me.

"Cool, tell her I said what's up. Don't go to your apartment tonight. Finish what you got to do and meet me at my crib. A nigga wants some shrimp alfredo and some pussy," I told her, placing her hand in mine and putting hers on my dick, so she could feel how hard my shit was.

She looked at me and burst out laughing. "You really think I'm about to give you some pussy after the shit you just pulled, having that bitch answer your phone? I'm about to start putting my foot down on you, Tez! No more having you fuckin' me, thinking that that will solve our problems. I make shit way too easy for you, so now I'm about to step shit up a notch. You keep claiming how much you love me, but show and prove, nigga."

"Damn, it's like that then?" I asked her, cocking my head to the side.

"Sure is," she shot back.

"Let's see if you still saying all of this shit tonight, once I get you in the bed with me. I'm serious about coming over, though. After I leave here, I got to make a few stops, and then I'll be home."

"Bye, Devontez," she said, trying to back out of my grasp, but I was holding onto her too tight.

"Give me a kiss first, and then I'll let you leave," I told her.

Shay leaned her head closer into mine and placed a nice, long juicy kiss on my lips. She allowed me to slide my tongue in her mouth and she slowly sucked on it. When I felt her moaning against my lips, I knew that all that talk she just did about holding out on the pussy was a bold face lie. We stayed wrapped up in our kiss for a few more seconds, and then she pulled away.

"Go ahead. I'll meet you at the house," I told her, and she nodded her head and walked away. I watched her hop in that Porsche I bought her that I think she loved more than my ass, and she took off.

"You silly in love ass nigga," my nigga Black called out to me. His nickname spoke for itself because the nigga was black as hell.

"You get you a bitch that do half the shit for you that mine does for me, and I'm sure you'll be in love too, nigga!" I shot back at him.

# CHAPTER 16

## Ashanti Palmer

*I* didn't want to say that I regret the day that I went behind Shonte's back and started fucking Chad, because that would be like me saying I regretted my baby, and Lord knows that wasn't the case at all. In fact, Ariel was the best thing to come from me and Chad's relationship, which had been a big lie from the beginning. Sometimes I found myself wondering if this man really even loved me. The way Shonte tried to fill the void with Chad since Jarvis was in prison, I kind of felt like he did the same thing with me. He knew that since Jarvis was back, that Shonte would run back to him, so in a way, I was just some sort of rebound for him. I never even thought about it that way because it was the first time ever that I finally had a man showing me a little bit of attention, so I took it and ran with it.

I'm not going to lie, though, I miss the hell out of Shonte and La'shay. Of course La'shay wasn't fuckin' with me either because of the shit that I did, and now it honestly felt like I had no one. Only people that I really had in my corner were my beautiful daughter and my mother. Chad was still staying here with me, but trust me, there was nothing romantic coming out of what him and I had going on. In fact, I needed to have a serious talk with him today about him moving out. There was no way that I would continue to let him to mooch off of me for free because he barely paid his side of the bills that he was supposed to pay. If I wanted a fuckin' roommate, I would have gone to college!

I was in the kitchen cleaning up when I heard my front door open. I peeked around the corner and noticed that it was Chad coming into the house. He had a defeated look on his face, as if he had the weight of the world on his shoulders. A part of me wanted to feel bad for him, but all of the heartache that he had caused just wouldn't allow me to.

He staggered into the kitchen where I was and then he took a seat in one of the high top chairs at the island. I stood before him and watched as he ran his hand over his face, and I knew right then that he was about to tell me some shit that I didn't want to hear.

"Ashanti, I know you may think that I don't love you, but honestly, I do. I think I love you more because you are my daughter's mother. You and I both know that this relationship thing that we had going on started on a fuckin' lie. I mean, I was fuckin' you so that you could give me inside information on Shonte. I'm not even going to sit here and try to fault you for catching feelings because honestly, I caught feelings as well, but it wasn't to the point where I knew that I wanted to spend the rest of my life with you. I know you may think that I still have some feelings for Shonte, but honestly, I'm not in love with her or no shit like that. But, yes, I still love her! I was with her for years. I even got down on my knees and asked her to marry me. That has nothing to do with what I'm about to tell you, I just felt the need to let you know that." He took a deep breath.

I watched him like a hawk because I was dying to hear this revelation.

"Damn, I don't even know how to say this shit without you judging me," Chad said and I heard his voice crack. *Is this nigga really about to cry?*

He looked up at me, and for the first time, I noticed that his eyes were bloodshot red, along with his nose. In fact, he had bags under his eyes and he looked like he hadn't slept in days.

"Chad, just tell me! It can't be that bad," I told him.

Hell, I hope it wasn't that bad.

"Ashanti, the reason why I can't be with you like that anymore is because for as long as I can remember, I've been having this constant battle with myself, trying to figure out just who the hell Chad Williams really is. With the way the world is, it's hard as hell to get acceptance from people since there is pretty much an unwritten rule on how people should and shouldn't be. I can't continue to run from these feelings, Ashanti, because I'm going to stress myself to death," he said, talking in circles.

I still didn't know where the hell he was trying to go with this damn story. I watched as tears fell from his eyes and he didn't even bother to wipe them. "I can't be the man that you want me to be, Ashanti, because I'm gay! There you go! I said it!" he said.

I didn't even know what to say, all I could do was hold my hand over my mouth and look at him with eyes filled with shock. For some reason, I was expecting to hear him tell me something about him getting another woman pregnant, but I never thought it would be this extreme. Immediately, I began to think about my health. *Damn. God, I know I fucked another bitch's man, but please, don't let AIDS or something like that be my karma.*

"You don't have anything, if that's what you're worried about," Chad said. It was almost as if he could read my mind. "If you love me like you say you did, Ashanti, then love me enough to not judge me because I'm about to be called every faggot and other stuff in the world, so please spare me. Also, I still want to be a part of Ariel's life, but I will no longer be living here with you. If you want to take it to the courts and figure out how we're going to co-parent, that's fine with me, but don't take my revelation to be a reason why you would take my daughter away from me," Chad told me, standing up from the chair.

I still hadn't uttered a word because I honestly didn't have a clue of what to say. I swear, I never would have thought he was gay. I just thought Chad was a pretty nigga since he didn't like to give head, but I never would have summed him up to be the type of nigga to take dick up the ass.

"You don't have to say nothing now. We'll talk," he told me and kissed my cheek then walked out of the apartment.

I knew that he was embarrassed, which is why he rushed his ass out of the apartment so fast. I wanted to say that I wouldn't judge him for how he lived his life, but how could I not? I felt like he had strung me along, and even though him and I were sleeping in separate rooms, I was kind of holding on to the hope that eventually we would get back together. I guess that would never happen because clearly he likes the same thing that I like, which is dick!

I already knew his mother was going to call him every name other than a child of God once she found out about her son's latest interest because she was so damn judgmental. She was so worried about me being a damn home wrecker when she had bigger fish to fry with her son.

After standing in the kitchen for a few more minutes, I grabbed my keys off of the table. Good thing my mom was watching Ariel tonight because Lord knows I needed a drink after the shit that Chad had just told me.

Fifteen minutes later, I pulled up to ABC Fine Wine & Spirits. I parked my car next to this bad ass Porsche truck. The tints on that bad boy were so dark that I couldn't tell whether someone was in there or not. I quickly shut my car off and then I got out, which was the biggest mistake on my part because not even a second later, the passenger side door opened.

"I promised you that when you had that baby I was going to be at your head!" Shonte told me, followed by a mean blow to my mouth.

I didn't even have time to recover from that blow because she landed another one in the same spot, causing blood to fly out of my mouth. I had to run my tongue over my top row of teeth because it felt like she had knocked a few teeth out.

"Wait... wait.... Let me just explain!" I tried to reason with her, but Shonte had turned into an animal as she continued to lay blow after blow on me.

I was now on my back, with her sitting on top of me, beating the shit out of my ass. I was in a state of shock right now, so I couldn't fight back even if I tried. I knew our time was coming when she and I would meet up again, but I honestly had been so busy with being a mom that I had completely forgotten about the beef that I had with Shonte.

"Shonte, let's go, bitch! Your ass is fuckin' pregnant. You beat her ass already!" La'shay said, trying to pull Shonte off of me.

A few minutes later, she was finally able to get her off of me. Shonte looked back at me as I held onto my side from when she had kicked me down on the ground. I had never got my ass beat like this in my life.

"Don't you even think that I beat your ass because of a nigga! I beat your ass because you went against the fuckin' code, Ashanti! You the same bitch that was smiling in my face, I even had your slut ass doing my fuckin' son's hair, when the whole time you were doing some messy shit like that behind my damn back! Rule of thumb, never let a nigga come between your friendship, especially not a nigga like Chad! Best believe that you were just some rebound pussy! I'm fuckin' you up on sight every time I see you because you're fuckin' disloyal," she spat at me and then she and La'shay jumped back into the truck and pulled off, leaving me there in pain.

My body felt like someone had rode over me with an 18 wheeler truck. *I got my ass beat for a nigga who turned out to be gay! Ain't this some shit?*

# CHAPTER 17

## *Shonte Howard*

"*G*irrlll, my brother is going to fuckin' kill you!" La'shay said, laughing as she drove like a bat out of hell from the parking lot.

I pulled down the sun visor and checked my face. Sure enough, I didn't have not one scratch on me. I know a lot of people are probably going to think I'm stupid for fighting that nothing ass bitch while I'm pregnant, but damn, I just couldn't let that moment slip through my fingers again. Truth be told, it wasn't even like Shay and I were following Ashanti or some shit; we just happened to be chilling in the parking lot because Shay had just run into the liquor store because while we were out, Tez had called and told her to pick him up some Patron.

I knew it was that bitch the moment she parked her car next to us. As soon as she stepped out of her car, I just attacked. Like I said earlier, I wasn't beating her ass for fucking Chad. It's just that loyalty was everything to me, and for her to pull some shit like that, I just had to lay hands on her. I wouldn't be able to sleep at night if I didn't.

"No he's not because you're not going to say shit!" I told La'shay. I swear if she told Jarvis on me, I would tell him some of her secrets that she had confessed to me over the years.

"It ain't me you need to be worrying about though. Did you not see them teenage boys out there recording the damn fight? Hoe, your wannabe Mayweather ass is probably going viral right now as we speak," Shonte said and laughed.

I'm glad her ass thought this shit was funny. That just goes to show that when I'm fighting, I'm in my own little zone because clearly I didn't see anybody with their phones out recording the fight.

About fifteen minutes later, La'shay pulled up to my house. I no longer had my apartment because I was now living with Jarvis. It served no purpose for me to continue paying rent over there if I was never there, so about two months ago, I moved out for good.

I looked at La'shay and I noticed that she didn't turn the car off. "You not getting out?" I asked her, taking off my seatbelt.

"Hell no, I'm not getting out! I'm not about to be in the middle of you and my brother's shit!" La'shay said.

I sucked my teeth and got out of her car, slamming the door behind me. I only wanted her to come in because I knew Jarvis wouldn't act that much of a fool with her around.

"Don't be mad at me, hoe! Call me later, well that's if Jarvis doesn't take your phone!" She laughed and then pulled out of the driveway.

I used my key and let myself in. The moment the door closed, my son took off running full speed in my direction. I picked him up and kissed him all over his face. At least with him home, I knew Jarvis wouldn't act all crazy. To be slick about the situation, I walked into the den area where Jarvis was sitting, with my son in my arms. Jarvis looked so fuckin' sexy sitting there in only his red and white Jordan basketball shorts, with no shirt on, showcasing his hard abs and all of the tattoos that adorned his stomach and arms. His head was freshly shaved and his goatee was perfect, just the way I liked it to be.

"Put him the fuck down, Shonte! I done already told you about carrying him around like that! Quit babying him, yo!" Jarvis snapped at me.

Between him and Kiondre, I didn't know who was worse because they always fussed at me about carrying Javari. I popped Javari out of me, so if I wanted to carry him, then I felt like I could do that. Funny thing is, I still put him down once Jarvis told me to.

"Javari, go in your room. Let me talk to your mama for a minute," Jarvis said.

"Why can't he stay down here?" I challenged.

I was only asking because I didn't want to be alone with Jarvis right now. I could tell he already knew what I had done. The shit was written all over his face. This is the part where I hated that everybody knew I was Jarvis's girl because I couldn't get away with shit without him finding out.

"Because I fuckin' said so, that's why! Javari, go upstairs to your room, and then I'll take you to your grandma's house," Jarvis said.

"Yayy," my son cheered and then he skipped up the stairs. Javari liked going over to Jarvis' mother's house because she let his lil' ass get away with murder.

"Come here for a second!" Jarvis beckoned me with his hand.

I slowly walked over to him, and once I was close enough, he sat me down on his lap. While I sat on his lap, he was bouncing his thigh that I was sitting on up and down, which was a sign that he was upset. I watched as he picked up his phone off the couch, typed in his passcode, which was my birthday, and then he went to his messages. He went to the message thread between him and Kiondre and opened the link that Kiondre had sent him.

About a second later, the link took him to the YouTube app and the title for the video was *Bad Ass Red Woman Beat the Shit Out of Another Woman in a Miami Plaza*. Jarvis played the video, and there I was on top of Ashanti, beating the shit out of her. I couldn't stand to watch the video, so I snatched the phone out of Jarvis's hand and then locked his phone.

"You must have forgot about when you were laid up in that hospital a few months ago after losing our baby. Every fuckin' night, I had to hold your ass while your cried yourself to sleep. You know all of this, so why the fuck would you go out and do some dumb shit that could bring harm to you and our baby, Shonte? Did you like that feeling when I came in the hospital that day and told you that you miscarried?" he asked, still staring at me with a pissed off look on his face.

"Jarvis, you know—"

"Answer my fuckin' question, Shonte! Did you like that feeling?" he asked me, causing the hairs on the back of my neck to stand up and for me to jump at the way he was talking to me.

"No, Jarvis, I didn't. But—"

"No fuckin' buts, Shonte! When you open your legs for me and I tell you that I want you to have my baby, I don't say that shit because it's some heat of the moment type of shit. I say it because it's the fuckin' truth! Stop doing dumb shit that will risk your chances of going full term with another baby that you're carrying for me. I know you wanted that bitch's head badly. I could see it in your eyes the way you looked at her when you saw her and that bitch ass nigga going to the doctor, but that shit could have waited. Listen to me and listen to me good, Shonte. You pull some shit like this again, I'm fuckin you up!" Jarvis told me.

I waved him off and wrapped my hands around his neck. I knew Jarvis would never in his life lay his hands on me again. He just wouldn't.

"You are so fuckin' sexy when you're mad," I told him, pulling his face to me and kissing him on his lips.

"Chill, I ain't even fuckin' with you like that right now," Jarvis said, trying to push me away from him, but I wasn't letting up.

I reached into his shorts and grabbed his big, meaty dick. "Oh, you not?" I asked him, jacking his dick and bringing my mouth up to his ear and running my tongue around it.

Jarvis couldn't resist me, just like how I couldn't resist him, so this little fake attitude that he had going on right now wouldn't last long once I put this pussy on him. Since I was wearing a nude colored maxi dress, I went ahead and pulled it up from the bottom and got comfortable in his lap. I pushed the thong that I was wearing to the side and slowly eased down on his dick; my dick. I loved riding Jarvis because this was the positon that got me anything I wanted. I could make him promise me the word at my fingertips while I was in this positon.

I heard Jarvis grunt beneath me and then he placed his large hands on my waist so he could guide my movements.

"I thought you wasn't fuckin' with me, daddy," I teased him as I spoke sexily into his ear.

That big dick pushing inside of me felt so fuckin' good. Since I've been pregnant, I think it was me who wanted the dick more than Jarvis, which was crazy because his ass wanted to fuck every second of the day.

"This pussy so fuckin' wet and tight, baby! Fuck is you... trying... to do to a niggaa? Fuck, man!" Jarvis said a little bit too loud.

I didn't want our son to catch us fuckin', so I removed my lips from his ear and placed them on his mouth so that I could stifle his loud outburst.

"I'm just trying to make sure you wasn't serious when you said you wasn't fuckin' with me anymore," I said into his lips as I continued to ride him nice and slow.

I swear sex with Jarvis was amazing, even if it was just a random quickie in the middle of the day. I placed my hands on his chest and threw my head back because he started lifting his hips under me and was fucking me harder. Now it was my turn to yell out.

"Fuccckkkk! Right there, baby!" I cried out as my eyes rolled to the back of my head. I was in pure euphoria right now as I took the quick strokes that he was handing out. "Goddddd... I'mmm cumminnn," I screamed and Jarvis placed his hands over my mouth. I seductively bit into it.

I knew he came too because I could fill his warm semen shooting up inside of me. After my body calmed down, I placed my head on his chest, still breathing heavily.

About five minutes later after I had calmed down, I asked him, "Why you sending Javari over to your mom's?" Not that I had a problem with it or anything, I just wanted to know.

"Our flight to Puerto Rico was supposed to be tonight, but now I don't know if I should take your ass, since you out fighting and shit!" Jarvis told me. Just that quick, his little attitude had come back.

"Puerto Rico? Baby pleaseeeeee. Don't cancel it now. I promise I won't do no dumb shit like that again," I pleaded with him, causing him to laugh at the desperation on my face. I had never been to Puerto Rico, and Jarvis knew how badly I wanted to go.

"You got almost four hours to get ready. Pack light though because I'm going to take you shopping when we get there," Jarvis told me, causing me to beam with pride.

"Thank you so much, baby," I said, showering his face with kisses.

I went upstairs to start getting ready. God, I couldn't wait to throw on a bikini and to put my feet in some Puerto Rican sand.

# CHAPTER 18

## Jarvis Banks

With all the crazy shit that was going on in Shonte's and my life, I felt like we needed to take a minute and regroup. For starters, I wasn't worried about Malaya because at the end of the day, there wasn't a nigga or a bitch alive that was about to pump any fear into my heart. Only thing I was worried about was her catching my girl or my son while I wasn't around, but then again, I knew Shonte had all the protection she needed just in case that bitch jumped crazy.

That day at my son's birthday party when she handed him a box of bullets with both my son and Shonte's name on it, was enough to send me over the edge. Not only did this hoe want my girl dead, but she was plotting on my lil man as well. I would never for the life of me understand how she could have only tasted my dick one time and she was causing all of this damn trouble. Imagine the shit her ass would have done had I fucked her. I swear the day I met up with her, it was going to be no talking; none of that because this bitch wasn't worth my energy. Truth be told, I don't care where I caught the bitch, when I eventually catch up to her, because Malaya is a hard one to find. When

I see her, it's definitely going to be lights out.

After being on a plane for almost three hours, we were finally landing in San Juan. I looked over at Shonte and her ass was knocked out, mouth open and all. I took a picture of her and then I quickly nudged her, telling her to get up.

"We're here," I told her, pulling the cover that she had on her lap off of her.

She opened her eyes and looked around. I couldn't sleep on planes because I didn't know anybody on this bitch except for Shonte, so I damn sure wasn't about to get caught slipping around a bunch of people I didn't know. I guess this was one of the many habits that I had picked up while doing my time in prison.

"Where your phone at?" I asked Shonte after we made our way off the plane.

We were sitting in first class, so we were one of the first to get off. I just couldn't do economy because I was a buff nigga and I needed my damn space.

"In my purse. Why, what happened?" she asked me.

"Deactivate your Facebook until we leave," I told her.

"What? How come? I wanted to take pictures while we are here," she told me with a pout on her beautiful face.

"Shonte, know that when I tell you to do something, it ain't because I'm trying to give you a hard time or to be an asshole about the situation. I ain't no dumb nigga, so I'm pretty sure Malaya popped up at Javari's birthday party because you posted a status saying where we were going. I don't need that bitch knowing that we are out of town and she try some slick shit while we're a thousand fuckin' miles away from our son. Deactivate the fuckin' page, Shonte, and you can upload your pictures when we get back!" I told her.

I didn't need to say anything else at that point because a few seconds later, she pulled her phone out of her purse and I watched as she opened the Facebook app and deactivated her page.

We finally made it inside the San Juan Luis Munoz Marin International Airport and I'll admit that this airport put Miami International airport to shame. The reason I picked Puerto Rico is because for one, Shonte had a picture of the beautiful beach as the wallpaper on her Mac desktop at home, and because she left the tab open when she was looking up things to do while in Puerto Rico. I felt like I wasn't making her smile as much as I should have, so two weeks ago is when I booked the trip.

Honestly, the plan was to just wake her ass up in the middle of the night and tell her to get ready, but when she started asking questions about why Javari was going over to my mom's, I knew then that I had to tell her.

"Ooohh baby, look at the bikinis over there. I want one," Shonte said, walking over to the store that they had in the middle of the airport with beach clothing.

I followed her over there and watched as she picked two out in her size and I met her at the register so that I could pay for them. Since I was planning for the two of us to do our shopping while we were there, we were able to skip baggage claim, since we both got on the plane with a carry on. It was harder than a muthafucka to get around this airport because the people that worked there barely spoke any English. We were finally able to ask someone where we needed to go so we could take a taxi to the hotel where we would be staying. Of course, the cab driver that pulled up and got us didn't speak a lick of English. Shonte swore the bullshit Spanish classes that she took in high school were enough for her ass to try and play interpreter.

Fifteen minutes later, we pulled up to the San Juan Marriott Resort & Stellaris Casino. It literally was right on the Condado beach, and I had to admit that this shit was indeed beautiful. I even had to pull my phone out and snap a few pictures myself. After tipping the driver, we made our way out of the taxi.

"Baby, this place is so beautiful," Shonte cooed as we turned around and looked at the beach.

We stood there for about five more minutes, just taking in the view, and then we walked into the hotel to check in. Funny how the last time I checked into a hotel with her things were different. She was engaged, which I knew was bullshit, and she kept swearing up and down that we were going to sleep in two separate rooms and that we weren't going to do anything while I had her in the hotel room with me. I laughed to myself because by midnight, I had her legs spread wide the fuck open and she kept telling me over and over again how much she loved a nigga. My dick got a little hard because I couldn't wait to fuck Shonte tonight on that balcony in our room as we looked out at the beautiful water and shit.

After checking in, we made our way all the way up to the Vice

Presidential suite, which was on the 26th floor of the hotel. When we opened the door to the room, I swear inside the room looked like something out of a damn movie. The room was beautifully decorated and it had everything that we would need, like a big spacious bedroom, which had a king bed in the middle of it, a dining room, living room and full kitchen. The windows were soundproof and floor to ceiling, and of course, my favorite part, which was the balcony.

"If my baby wasn't back home, I swear I would say that I never want to leave this room," Shonte said, plopping down on the bed.

As she lay there, my eyes went down to her stomach, which had a little bump now, so you could most definitely tell that she was pregnant. Shonte had always been beautiful to me. Shit, I say it all the time, but it was something different about her beauty when she was carrying my child.

"You know I love you, right?" I said, walking over to her and pulling her up from the bed.

"I know you do. You planning this trip for me proves your love for me," she told me, wrapping her arms around me and kissing my lips.

"You know I would do anything to make you smile right?" I asked her.

I normally wasn't this romantic type of nigga, but being around Shonte for all of these years, she had a way of bringing my soft side out.

"I know you will. You've been making me smile since I was fifteen years old, Jarvis," she told me.

"Alright, I just want you to know that you mean the world to me,

Shonte. I swear to God, you do," I told her, cuffing her face in my hands.

I watched as her eyes got watery. "Chill, chill, I ain't mean to make your cry," I told her, using my fingers to wipe her eyes.

"It's happy tears, baby," she told me through her tears.

I loved this woman way too much to go another day without doing what I know needed to be done a long time ago. I knew from the day that I met Shonte that I wanted her to be my wife, so it was no sense in prolonging the situation.

### Later that night

I fucked up when I told Shonte that I would take her shopping once we arrived in Puerto Rico. I kid you not, we left the hotel this afternoon around one, and here it was going on ten o'clock, and we were just now walking back into the suite. I knew that before we left, I was going to have to buy her a suitcase to carry all of this unnecessary shit that she had made me purchase at the mall. While we were out, I copped some weed. Kiondre had been here before with his girl, so he told me where to go and get some of the best weed here in Puerto Rico.

While Shonte was in the suite doing God knows what, I stood on the balcony getting higher than a muthafucka. Who would have ever thought that a hood ass nigga such as myself would be able to afford some luxury shit like this to take my girl? Back when I was younger, I only dreamed of being able to do some of the shit that I was able to do now. Not only that, but I was able to spoil my girl rotten and still make my money the legal way. I thanked God every day for my success because without him, none of this shit would be possible.

I was leaned over the rail, smoking, and letting the sounds of the ocean take me away when all of a sudden, I heard some heels clicking behind me. I quickly put my blunt out because it was stupid thing to be smoking around the woman who was carrying my child. I turned around and admired the sexy little negligee that Shonte was wearing. It literally left little to the imagination because I had a perfect view of her sexy titties that sat up nicely. If she were to turn around, I know for a fact that I would be able to see her ass hanging out of the see through lace that she was wearing.

"You like it, daddy?" she asked me, putting her finger in her mouth and turning around for me, so that I was able to see the whole thing.

Just as I imagined, all of her ass was hanging out, and I just had to reach my hand out and slap it one good time. All of that ass that she had back there, and it was real too.

"You already know I like that shit. You coming out here half naked, you must be trying to fuck or something," I told her, pulling her body into mine.

Damn, she smelled so fuckin' good. I ran my hands through her burgundy hair, which I had fallen in love with the moment my eyes landed on her that day at the restaurant for my little welcome home party. For years, Shonte's hair was long and jet black, so it was surprising to see that she had cut her hair into a bob, but nonetheless, the shit was sexy as fuck to me.

"I am trying to fuck. I want to suck your dick first, though."

It was almost as if my dick could hear what she said because within seconds, it was damn near trying to burst out of the polo shorts that I was wearing.

"Do your thang then, baby," I said, kissing her lips and then placing my elbows on the railing behind me.

I could hear people under us at the beach, but I wasn't worried about them seeing us because it was dark as fuck where we were. I knew in a few minutes they were about to be listening to some exclusive fucking once I slid my dick up in Shonte, though. I looked down at her as she slowly got down on her knees and unbuckled the shorts that I was wearing. She didn't even bother pulling them all the way down because she was in such a hurry to get all of this dick in her waiting mouth.

"No hands! Make that shit nasty how I like it!" I demanded, reaching my hand over and slapping her on her ass.

Shonte placed both of her small hands on my waist, and with her tongue, she was able to lift my dick up and place it in her mouth. She was sucking me nice and slow, but it was nasty as fuck because she kept taking my dick out of her mouth, spitting on it, and trying to force the whole damn thing down her throat.

I couldn't take all of that teasing, so I reached down, placed my hands on either side of her face, and started fuckin' her mouth. "You better not gag either!" I demanded.

I watched as her eyes began to water, but she still kept sucking that dick. "Fuck! Damn girl!" I kept grunting.

I swear, after tonight, I was about to start calling her super head because she was literally a beast right now with the way she had a nigga clenching my ass cheeks together and curling my damn toes.

"Fuccckkk, I'ma nut!" I growled, and like the good girl that she was, she kept sucking me and allowed me to bust in her mouth.

"Take all of that shit off right now, but leave on the shoes! Face the water and put your leg up here!" I said, pointing to the table that was on our patio.

Shonte quickly removed the negligee that she was wearing and she went over to the railing, placed her hands on it and propped her leg up on the table. My dick was still hard, so I creeped up behind her and slid inside her. Immediately, her body tensed up and she reached back and tried to push me away.

"Don't move! Let me feel it, baby," I told her, reaching around and holding her tender breasts in my hands.

"Jarvissss... they gonna hear me babbyyy... Fuccckkkk," she cried out.

She was referring to the people down at the water. I honestly didn't give a fuck because it wasn't like they could see us or some shit.

"Fuck them people! Worry about taking this dick!" I told her and then bit her on her shoulder.

I was balls deep in the pussy, and purposely trying to make her scream out loud for me. Only thing that could be heard on our balcony was the sound of my dick slamming into her pussy, and Shonte's sexy ass moans mixed with her cries.

"Ohhh, babyyy... you on my spot!! Fuckkkk, I love you so much baby," she kept telling me over and over again.

"I know you do, bae! I love you too! Cum on my dick!" I said against her neck, with my arm wrapped tightly around her waist.

When I felt her movements slow down, I knew then that she was about to cum, and I was right behind her. I picked her body up, sat down on one of the chairs, and I let Shonte ride me. We went at it for another thirty minutes, and when I felt her body collapse against me, I knew then that she was out for the night. I carried her back into the suite and placed her body on the bed. She was knocked out, so I placed a kiss on her forehead and went to take a shower.

When I finished showering, I threw on a pair of clean boxers and walked back into the room. I went over to the nightstand where I had hidden the ring, pulled out the box that I had gotten from Jared two weeks ago, and took the massive ring out. While Shonte slept, I lifted up her left hand and placed the ring on her ring finger. Y'all should know by now that I wasn't your regular ass nigga. I knew the moment Shonte opened her eyes in the morning, she would feel all of that weight on her hand, and I would be awakened by her screams once she saw what I had done.

Lord knows that this moment was way overdue. It's official, I couldn't go another day without making this woman my wife. She had proven to me a long time ago that she was the one I wanted to give my last name to. Now, I just needed to hope and pray that she said yes.

# CHAPTER 19

## Shonte Howard

*I* woke up the next morning with a bad ass headache and an aching ass pussy. I had given Jarvis' ass rounds last night, and now my body was repaying me for it. I reached over and grabbed one of the pillows and placed it between my legs, hoping that it would stop some of the throbbing that I had going on down there. When I went to pick the pillow up, something felt different on my hand. I looked at my hand and noticed that I had a massive ass 14k white gold diamond ring on my finger. Clearly I was tripping. I know for sure that this wasn't on my finger when I went to sleep last might.

I closed my eyes and opened them up again because maybe I was dreaming or something. But when I opened them again, the ring was still sitting beautifully on my finger.

"Oh my, God! Oh my, God!" I kept repeating over and over, followed by a scream.

I jumped up from the bed because Jarvis was no longer lying there with me and took off in search of him in this big ass suite. I found him a few seconds later and he was in the kitchen down on one knee.

Immediately, tears came to my eyes because I knew then that this wasn't a joke at all.

"Come closer," Jarvis told me.

I walked over to him with my hands over my mouth and tears silently falling from my eyes. When I was close enough to him, he pulled me into him by my waist and sat me down on his knee.

"I gave you that ring because you deserve it. I'll admit that they way I treated you back then was wrong. Lord knows that I would take a nigga's head off if they ever were to fuck with my daughter's heart the way that I did yours. Even with all of the shit that I was doing back then, I knew that I loved you, I just had a fucked up way of showing it. I always felt like I was missing something, when you were all a nigga really needed in the end. You gave me a son, you're carrying another baby for me, you're doing all of the shit right now that I dreamed of you doing when I first met you. Will you marry me, Shonte?" Jarvis asked me, looking me dead in my eyes.

For years, I had dreamt of this moment. Now that it was finally happening, I couldn't even find the words to say because I couldn't stop myself from crying.

"Yes," I managed to get out through my tears. I wrapped my arms around Jarvis's neck and held onto him for dear life.

"Let's go get married right now, baby. Come on, you and me," Jarvis told me.

I had to remove my arms and look at him because I wanted to know if he was serious or not. Don't get me wrong, I had no problem with eloping because the quicker he made me his wife, the better.

"Seriously, baby? Like today?" I asked him after I had finished crying.

"I'm dead ass serious, Shonte. If you want to do a big ass wedding when we get home that's fine, but come on baby, let me make you my wife today," Jarvis pleaded.

It really wasn't a point in him begging because I was down no matter what.

"What would we wear? Where would we even go?" I asked once the two of us had stood up from the floor.

"You trust me?" he asked me, looking down at me.

"Of course I do," I told him.

"Alright then. Leave everything to me. Only thing you have to worry about is showing up," Jarvis told me and placed a kiss on my lips. If it wasn't even possible, I swear I had fallen in love all over again.

Not even a whole four hours later, I went from being Ms. Shonte Howard to Mrs. Shonte Banks. Most people probably feel that Jarvis and I rushed things, but how could this moment possibly have been rushed when I've loved him for over fifteen years? I'm not going to lie, every girl dreamed of having that big fairytale wedding, but what made Jarvis and my ceremony so special, which only consisted of him, myself, and the preacher, was the fact that nothing was planned.

I'm not even sure that Jarvis had the whole idea of him and I eloping in Puerto Rico planned because he didn't even pack clothes for the wedding ceremony, let alone pick something out from the mall yesterday when we were there damn near all day. I was already prepared for the tongue lashing that my mother, as well as Jarvis' mother was going to put on me once they found out that we went and got married without them in attendance. I'm pretty sure that the two of them would have wanted to be there to witness that beautiful moment, since they were the two women who gave us to each other.

I was laid up in the bed after making love to my husband, when my phone started to ring. I grabbed my phone of the nightstand and noticed that it was my mother calling me.

"Hey, Mommy," I answered with a huge smile plastered on my face. Ever since this morning, I just couldn't stop smiling.

"Hey, I know you're on vacation, Shonte, but somebody came to my house looking for you. She said it was important," my mom told me.

Immediately, I began to panic because who the fuck could possibly be looking for me, and why the hell would they pop up at my parents' house?

"Who was it? Did they leave a name? I asked, sitting up in the bed.

I could feel Jarvis' eyes burning a hole through me. I assumed he wanted to know what the hell was going on.

"No, she didn't leave a name, she just said that it was important," my mom said.

"Damn, ma, why didn't you ask for her name? How did she look?" I asked, this time getting out of bed and pacing back and forth. I had a feeling as to who it was that had the balls to pop up at my mother's house looking for me.

"Because when I asked her for her name, she told me that she would just come back, and she left! She was dark skinned, with burgundy hair, and—"

"Shit!" I cursed because just like I had assumed, it was Malaya who had popped up at my mother's house.

"What's wrong, Shonte? You know her or something?" my mom asked me. I could hear the panic in her voice.

"Look out the window and see if her car is still there," I told my mom.

"No, she left about five minutes ago! Shonte, what the fuck is going on? What aren't you telling me?" my mom screamed into the phone. I knew she had to be pissed because my mom never cursed like that.

"Ma, that bitch is fuckin' dangerous! She's the one who caused me to lose my baby! She has this crazy infatuation with Jarvis, and the bitch is not going to stop until me and my son are dead. I have no idea why she went over to your house, though, but Ma, do not answer the door for her again because the bitch is crazy."

I was pissed off now because here I was thousands of miles away from home, and if this bitch wanted to harm my parents right now, she could. Just the thought of something happening to my parents scared the shit out of me. After I talked to my mom for a few more minutes, she and I hung up the phone and I ran down to Jarvis everything that had just happened.

"You already know what this means. Pack your shit, we got to cut this trip short," Jarvis told me.

149

Immediately, we started packing our bags so that we could head back home. There was no way in hell that I would be able to relax and enjoy Puerto Rico when we had a crazy bitch at home lurking the streets. It's no telling how many times this bitch has rode past my parents' house.

# CHAPTER 20

# *Malaya Brown*

*I* needed to start back taking my medicine because I was going to fuck around and get myself killed making the wrong moves. This was the second time that I had come to Shonte's parents house, but it was the first time that her mom had actually opened the door, since no one was home the first time. I was low key being sloppy with my shit because what the fuck would I have done if I had popped up over there and Shonte was home?

I was just so mad because I'm normally able to know Shonte's whereabouts because her stupid ass posts everything on Facebook. For the past three days, I had been trying to look at her page, but each time I typed in her Facebook name, it wouldn't show up, so I assume she must have deleted it. The plan was for me to go over to her parents' house, pretend that I was a friend of Shonte's, and somehow try to get her mother to tell me where she was. But the moment I opened my mouth and told her that I was Shonte's friend, she looked at me funny, like she didn't believe me or something. Right then, I knew I had to get the fuck out of dodge, especially when she asked me for my name.

Truth is, I had stopped taking my medicine a few months ago because I didn't like the way it made me feel. But when I didn't take it, I did things that I normally wouldn't do, like killing four people in less than one year. I didn't even know what sleep is anymore because lately I've been having nightmares like a muthafucka. At night, all I would see is images of Tank, Mya, Justin, my mom, and Deon standing over me with blood pouring out of their bodies. They would be holding conversations with me, constantly asking me why I took their life.

Not much scared me, but I'm not going to lie, that shit right there did something to me. I constantly found myself trying to fight them and their voices away. Right now, I was laid up in bed watching TV my phone rang with a number that I had never seen before. I declined the call, but it kept right on ringing. Sensing that the caller wasn't going to let up until I answered it, I finally accepted the call.

"Who the fuck is this?" I asked, sitting up in the bed.

"That's how you pick up the phone for a nigga?" his sexy, deep ass voice boomed through the line.

My panties got a little wet at the sound of his voice because it had been so long since I'd heard him. I see him just about every day since I'm always parked in front of his recreation center.

"I'm sorry, I didn't know that it was you," I said with a goofy smile on my face. I knew sooner or later that he would be calling me to see what this pussy was all about.

"Listen, I want to meet up with you sometime tonight. You think you'll be free?" he asked me.

Months ago, I would have died to hear him ask me some shit like this, but now it was different. I knew that he was aware that I was after his bitch and his son, so right now, he was trying to get me before I got him. I may be labeled insane, but I wasn't fuckin' crazy. It's fine, though, I'll play the dummy role if that's what he wanted me to do.

"Sure, when and where?" I said

"Alright, cool. Meet me over there at Bunch Park around eight," he told me, causing me to laugh out loud.

Did this nigga really think that I would be caught dead in that area where it was no fuckin' lights, so he could do God knows what to me? Hell no, I don't think so!

"How about you meet me at Texas Roadhouse over in Miramar around eight? See you then," I told him and hung up the phone.

I chose this spot because I knew that the parking lot was always deep with police, so whatever wicked plan he had in mind wouldn't go down tonight. The fact that this man tried to get me to meet up with him at one of the most dangerous parts of town left no doubt in my mind that he had plans to kill me tonight.

A few minutes before eight o'clock that night, I pulled up to Texas Roadhouse. If I must say so myself, I looked damn good. Jarvis would be a fuckin' fool to pass all of this up with the way that I was wearing this dress tonight. After parking my car, I got out and walked inside, letting the hostess know that I was waiting for someone else to join me.

About ten minutes later, Jarvis walked into the building, and it was almost like the cologne he wore wafted throughout the whole room. This man was just too fuckin' fine for words, and it made me realize just why in the hell I was doing all of this to get with him. He walked into the restaurant, casually dressed in a pair of white True Religion jeans and a striped, red and white polo. On his feet were a pair of white and red Air Jordan 12's that were just released not too long ago. Of course he was wearing his Cuban around his neck, and his head was freshly shaved.

I couldn't help but to think nasty thoughts of having his goatee drenched in my juices as he had my legs spread eagle while he feasted on my pussy. I had to cross my legs because my clit was literally thumping from looking at him too hard.

"You checked in already?" he asked once his eyes landed on me. No hug or nothing; clearly this nigga wasn't here to play any games with my ass.

"Yes," I told him.

After about five more minutes, my name was called. The hostess walked us to a table outside, since that's where I told them that I would like to sit.

I saw the police officers in the parking lot, so I wanted Jarvis to know that if he planned to do something stupid, his ass would be in jail tonight.

After the waitress set the bread down on the table, she took our drink order and let us know that she would be back soon to take our order for dinner. The whole time that she was talking to us, I could feel the hateful look that Jarvis was giving me, and it honestly made me nervous. After she left, Jarvis reached under the table, placed his hand on the edge of the wooden chair that I was sitting in and roughly pulled me closer to him direction. That act alone was enough for me to swallow hard and look at him with nervous eyes.

"The thing that's pissing me off with you, Malaya, is the fact that I never fuckin' led you on! Yeah, I let you suck my dick out in public, but let's be real, any bitch can get down on her knees and suck my dick. But does that mean I give a fuck about them? You don't even know what it feels like to have the head of my dick even tickle your pussy, so I'm having a hard fuckin' time coming to grips with why you going so hard for some dick that you don't even know what the fuck it feels like! I came to you as a man. I told you that what you and I had going on, that shit was going to end because I was getting back with my baby mama! I never disrespected your ass or called you out of your fuckin' name, even when you did come off as being a hoe! Yet, you turn around, set a fuckin' dog on my girl and cause her to miscarry. Not only that, but I know for a fact that it was you who killed my son!" Jarvis said, all in a harsh whisper.

*Whew, I love when a man puts me in check! That shit was so fuckin sexy to me!*

I didn't know what to do, so the only thing left was for me to laugh in his face. Did he honestly think I gave a fuck about his bitch losing that damn baby? Fuck no, I didn't! I'll do that shit all over again if I had to.

With lighting speed, Jarvis hopped up from the table and wrapped his hands around my throat, squeezing the shit out of it. I tried to pry his hands away from me, but his crazy ass wouldn't let up.

"That's exactly how I'm going to laugh when I watch my bitch hold that gun to your head and blow your fuckin' brains out! You think

I give a fuck about them cops sitting in that damn car? You think them muthafuckas going to protect your silly ass? You won't even dare go to them for help because you got too many bodies on your hands to even fuck with them! I'm not even about to make any threats to your crazy ass, just know that me and my bitch are ready for whatever it is that you got planned. You think you crazy, Malaya, but I'm bat shit crazy!" Jarvis grimaced in my ear and then he pushed me hard as hell, leaving me to fall on the floor.

Everyone outside was looking at me crazy, while Jarvis stepped over me and walked out of the gate that led to the parking lot, like he didn't just choke me out in a room full of people. Funny thing is, the police never came over to check and see if I was okay, nor did they even arrest his black ass for doing what he had just done to me!

# CHAPTER 21

## Shonte Banks

*I*t was Saturday morning, and Jarvis, Javari, La'shay, Devontez, myself, and Jarvis's mom were all at Cracker Barrel having breakfast. I don't know what the hell was going on with Jarvis, but he had been tense ever since he came back home last night. I had been with Jarvis long enough to know that whatever was bothering him, he would never just come right out and tell me, even if I begged him to. He would do it when he was good and damn ready. All I knew was that he left the house last night and told me not to wait up for him. Of course, I waited up, and when he got back home, which was a little after ten o'clock, he had been on edge ever since.

I kept asking him what happened, but he wouldn't even tell me, which was pissing me off. Jarvis hated when I kept secrets from him, yet, here he was doing the very thing to me that he hates for me to do to him.

We've been back from Puerto Rico for two weeks, and I haven't had the chance to let anybody know that Jarvis and I were married. It wasn't that I was scared to say something, it's just that I hadn't gotten around to doing it yet. As I flipped through the menu to see what I wanted to eat for breakfast, La'shay grabbed my left hand and started to examine the ring on my finger.

"Umm, never mind the fact that you are blinding me and everybody else in this bitch with this ring, but what is this? When did this happen?" La'shay asked, being her normal, dramatic self.

I looked at Jarvis for confirmation and he nodded his head, telling me to go ahead and tell them.

"We... umm... we got married in Puerto Rico," I said, stumbling all over my words because I was scared of the way that Jarvis' mom was looking at me.

"What?" Both La'shay and Regina asked me in unison.

"Jarvisss," I whined because I didn't want to be the one doing all of the dirty work, and he wasn't making the situation any better with his silence.

"This is my wife, y'all! I proposed to her in Puerto Rico, she said yes, and we eloped while we were on vacation," Jarvis said and then pulled me into him, placing a rough kiss on my cheek. Then he went back to looking over the menu.

"Bitch, y'all been back for two weeks and I'm just now finding out about this? See if I tell your ass any more of my secrets," La'shay said, making me laugh.

"Your ass ain't got no damn secrets to be telling in the first place," Tez told La'shay.

"As long as I'm with you, trust me, I'm always going to have a fuckin' story to tell, with your cheating ass!" she shot back at him.

I was dying laughing. The two of them were fuckin' clowns, and they reminded me so much of Angela and Marcus from *Why Did I Get Married?* because they were constantly going back and forth. I thought Jarvis and I were bad, but clearly the two of them put the icing on the cake. All Tez did was shake his head and continue looking over the menu.

"But congratulations anyway. I'm happy for you two," La'shay told me.

Regina congratulated us as well, even though I knew she felt some type of way, she just didn't voice it yet. After everybody ordered their food, we all sat around talking.

"Ma, look! There goes my other daddy!" Javari said.

I looked up at the door to see Chad walking in with another fine ass man, one whom I had never seen him with before.

"What? Javari, don't call that man your fuckin' daddy!" Jarvis snapped at my son.

Javari stood up from his seat crying and jumped into my lap, burying his head in my chest. I knew his feelings were hurt by the way Jarvis had just snapped on him and he was embarrassed. I also knew Jarvis well enough to know that he regretted doing that the moment he realized what had come out of his mouth.

Jarvis had never raised his voice at Javari like that, even when he deserved to be yelled at. Jarvis snatched Javari out of my lap and placed him in his. I watched as he apologized for raising his voice at him and then he told Javari to go sit back in his seat and he did.

"Can't believe you had my son calling that bitch ass nigga daddy!" Javris snapped at me in a low whisper.

I didn't even bother responding to him because then we would be arguing in this restaurant in front of everybody. Chad still had yet to see us, but best believe my eyes were trained on him. I wasn't even looking at him because I missed him or anything, but something was off with him. I mean, the way he carried himself around his friend was different, even the way he dressed was a little unusual as well. The skinny jeans that he was wearing were tighter than the jeans I had on right now. *What the fuck! Is this nigga gay or something?*

"You sure know how to pick them! Dick in the booty ass nigga!" I heard Jarvis grumble.

"Says the nigga that was fuckin' with a bitch who caused me to lose my baby!" I snapped on him because he had no room to talk.

"Shonte, what the fuck is wrong with this picture right now? Is Chad gay?" La'shay asked me.

I mean, I didn't want to jump to conclusions, but clearly I was the third person at the table who had assumed this. I was staring at Chad so hard that eventually he looked over at me, and I could see the embarrassment all over his face. Not even two seconds later, he told his friend something and they both stood up to leave. That alone proved to me that I was truly indeed, once open a time fuckin' a dick in the booty ass nigga!

I suddenly got a funny taste in my mouth and I hightailed it to the bathroom, throwing up the two biscuits that I had just ate at the table while we were waiting on our food. How could I not have known that I was dating a gay man? Let alone, engaged to him. I was so embarrassed right now that I didn't even want to come out of the bathroom stall. About two minutes later, I heard the bathroom door open and then close.

"Shonte, open the door" La'shay said, gently knocking on the stall that I was in.

I was in handicapped stall, so there was more than enough room for her and I to be in there at the same time. When I opened the door for her, she looked at me with a funny expression on her face.

"Shay, this shit is so fuckin' embarrassing, man! How could I not have known?" I cried, slumping down to the floor and wiping my eyes.

"Shonte, don't blame his sexuality on you! You didn't fuckin know," she told me, sitting beside me on the floor and wrapping her arms around me.

"God, this shit all makes sense now," I said, laughing through my cries. "Him always wearing condoms with me, the fact that he didn't like to give oral, and it was like he was mad all of the fuckin' time. Here I was thinking it was something that I was doing wrong, when all along, this nigga was just trying to find himself," I told La'shay.

"I'm not even going to lie, if that's his boyfriend, that nigga is fine as fuck," La'shay said, making me laugh.

I don't know why I even cared to think about her, but I wondered if Ashanti knew about Chad being gay. Shit, she probably did, and that's why her ass was at the liquor store the day I beat her ass. The bitch probably needed something strong after finding out about his little secret. Boyyyy, I swear. Karma was a muthafucka because the same nigga that she so called took from me didn't even like anything that her or I had to offer him.

After finally getting myself together, Shay and I stood up from the floor and we went back to the table with everybody else. Just as we took out seats, the waitress came over and placed our food on the table. I couldn't even bring myself to eat because I was still in a state of shock after seeing Chad and that man together.

# CHAPTER 22

## *Chad Williams*

$\mathcal{F}$or some odd reason, I was more afraid of Shonte finding out about me than my own mother. At the end of the day, Shonte and I were together for years before we called it quits, so her opinion really mattered to me. When we were at the restaurant and my eyes landed on her, I swear I felt like shit. Her eyes didn't hold any signs of judgment, more like hurt, anger, and confusion. Her baby daddy on the other hand, he looked like he was calling me every faggot in the damn book, with his fine ass.

I had already knew that I was somewhat on the down low, but I knew the shit was for real when I came into contact with Jarvis at the Easter dinner a while back. I wasn't crazy though, I knew that he would probably fuckin' kill me if I made a move on him. Two months after that, I met Tony. It was just something about his whole vibe. I had never felt that way while being around a woman, not even Shonte, and I loved the ground she walked on. What was so special about Tony was that he wasn't trying to hook up with me for the wrong reasons, nor was he pressing me to come out about my sexuality, even though he already knew I was gay. He said that he could just tell.

What started off as friends, led to him being the first man that I had ever been sexually involved with, and I honestly loved every moment of it. Having sex with a woman was okay, but a man, myyyy Goddddd! If I knew it would feel that good, I would have explored my feelings a long time ago. Even with all of that, I still hadn't come around and told my mother yet, but I owed it to Ashanti to tell her. At the end of the day, she had my baby, so I couldn't leave her blind.

That day when I walked in on her and confessed to being a gay man, I couldn't stand to watch the anger in her eyes that she held for me, which is why I quickly got out of there. Since then, I've moved in with Tony and everything was going well, but I knew shit was about to take a turn for the worse. I'm pretty sure that he will want to know why I had us storm out of the restaurant when we were only seated for about five minutes.

"What the fuck was that all about, Chad?" Tony asked me the moment he got behind the wheel of his Camaro and pulled out of the parking space.

I watched as the muscles in his jaw kept twitching, which only proved to me how livid he was.

"That was her," I told him.

"Who the fuck is her? Who was that, Chad? What was so fuckin' bad that it caused you to fuck up us having breakfast?" he asked me.

"That was Shonte," I told him.

Tony knew all about Shonte. There was nothing that I didn't tell Tony because I felt comfortable enough to tell him things, so there were never any secrets between him and I.

"So you leave? You keep talking about how ready you are to come out, but when you get in public, you do immature shit like this! How the fuck you think it makes me feel when we go out in public and I try to hold your hand and you push me away? Chad, if you're not ready for all of this, let me fuckin' know now, and I will leave you alone! How many more times do I have to tell your ass that I am not about to keep a man that doesn't want to be kept?" Tony barked.

I let what he said marinate in my mind for a little bit. I knew then that this was the moment that I needed to man the fuck up and do what I had to do. If I loved this man the way that I claimed, then I would show and prove.

"Take that exit right there," I told him, pointing to exit 47 as we were on the highway.

"What's that way?" Tony asked me.

"Just take the exit, Tony!" I told him.

He put on his turn signal so that he could take the exit.

I showed him where to go, and in about ten more minutes, we pulled up in front of my mother's house. This right here would definitely prove my love to him because my mother was the most judgmental person in this damn world. I was prepared though, for whatever had to come after this. If me being gay was too much for her to handle, then I was willing to walk away from her today and never have to come into contact with her ever again. The world was already about to judge me, so I didn't need the woman who gave me life judging me as well.

I had Tony pull the car up in the driveway, and I waited a few more seconds, praying to God and asking him for strength to get through this. We both got out of the car and I walked up to the doorstep and then rang the doorbell. About a minute later, my mother came to the door. The smile that was once on her beautiful face quickly went away the moment her eyes landed on Tony and I.

My mother wasn't a dumb woman, so I assumed that she already knew what was up, especially since I stood there holding hands with my lover. I tried to put on this facade of confidence, but the truth is, I wanted to run under a rock and die because this was just all too much for me. But my love for Tony just wouldn't let me walk away.

"Can we come in?" I asked my mother. As I talked, my voice shook because I was so damn nervous.

My mom didn't even respond, she just opened the door wide enough for us and then she let us in. The whole way to the den, I held onto Tony's hand, but when we sat down, I let go of it. Tony and I sat on the couch, while my mother sat in front of us on the loveseat. I fiddled with my fingers for a little while, a habit that I'd picked up over the years whenever I was caught in an uncomfortable situation.

"Soo, Ma, this is Tony. Tony, this is my mother," I said, introducing the two.

"And who is Tony to you?" my mom asked, not even bothering to shake Tony's hand when he reached out to her.

She looked at his hands as if he had the plague or something and then she nastily focused her attention back on me. My mother is really a nasty woman, but she could be nice when she wanted to be. I'm not quite sure, but I think her nasty attitude is what drove my father away.

Didn't matter to me because I don't think my father cared too much about me in the first place. It was almost as if he saw something in me that everyone else didn't see, and it caused him to hate me. Because of that, I hadn't seen his ass in years.

Now, I wondered if he was able to tell that I was gay back then, and because of that, it caused him to go astray. Truth be told, I haven't seen my father since I was five years old, and that was when he beat the shit out of me because he caught me in my mother's bathroom playing in her makeup kit. Like I said, I've been battling with my feelings for years, but it took Tony coming into my life for me to realize that I needed to accept that I was indeed a gay man.

After letting the question that my mother just asked me replay in my head for a little while longer, I finally looked up at her and answered. "Tony is my boyfriend, Ma. For years, I've been trying to convince myself and everyone else around me that I could do this whole *straight* thing, but I just can't. I knew at a very young age that I was different, and I'm pretty sure you did too, but you never spoke on it. I was engaged, Ma, to one of the most beautiful woman to ever grace this planet, but her beauty wasn't enough to stop these feelings that I had inside of me for other men.

"When I met Tony a while back, we were friends. Everything that I was missing with Shonte, I found with him. I almost felt like I was complete now that he is in my life. I said almost complete because I know that I don't have your blessing, which is why I'm coming to you now as a man to let you know the changes that have been going on in my life," I told my mother.

The entire time that I spoke, Tony rubbed my back because he knew how tough this was on me. As I sat there and poured my heart out to my mother, she looked as if nothing I said had moved her. In fact, I'm one hundred percent sure that if she had a gun on her, she probably would have killed my ass and Tony.

"And you will never have my fuckin' blessing, Chad!" my mom barked at me.

We sat in silence for a few more minutes and then she finally let out a hurt filled laugh. I said hurt because I could look in her eyes and see the emotions that she had going on right now, the biggest one being regret. I don't know what she was regretful of, but I'm pretty sure that I was going to find out.

"Your daddy was right all along, but I just didn't want to believe him! I remember when you were five, and your daddy caught you playing in my makeup. He beat the shit out of you. Even prior to that, he kept telling me that he thought you were gay because you never liked to do any manly shit around the house. I simply shrugged it off because you were a baby then, you didn't know shit about being gay. Now, years later, and your father was right all along," she said.

I watched as one lone tear escaped from her eye, but she quickly wiped it away. "It was because of you that your father left me alone for all of these years and forced me to be this bitter woman. You drove your fuckin' father away, Chad, and now you come in here with your faggot friend and expect me to give you my fuckin' blessing on a gay ass relationship. What the fuck is wrong with you? You were raised in the fuckin' church, Chad! How do you go from fuckin' two women, to now taking dick up the ass?" my mother barked.

That was enough for me to get up out of my seat and jump in her face. I understood that she was hurt, hell I was hurting too, but there was no need for her to be disrespectful right now. Then she wants to sit up here and blame my father's leaving on me when clearly his ass was looking for any opportunity to leave. Who would have ever thought that she would blame me for what that nigga did?

"Ma, I love you, and your blessing is greatly needed, but if I'm not going to get one from you, that's fine. However, you will fuckin' respect me. There's a lot of shit that you do and say that I don't agree with, but I will never come out of my mouth and say anything close to as hurtful as what you just said to me. I was already mentally prepared for the way that you would react on the drive over here, but this is over the top, even for you. Let me know right now what's it's going to be because I've lived my life long enough trying to do things that are expected of me, and never doing things that make Chad happy. If you can't accept me being gay, then clearly, you can't accept me for who I am," I told her.

I never thought that I would have to dish out an ultimatum to my own damn mother, but she had forced this.

"When I get that phone call at twelve in the morning, telling me that you just died from AIDS, it'll be too late then for you to know why you'll never get my blessing on anything that has to do with you dating a man," she told me.

I nodded my head, letting her words play in my mind. That comment right there was way below the belt, but I had no choice but to respect it.

"Goodbye, Ma," I told her, then leaned down and kissed her on her forehead one last time.

I walked over to Tony, grabbed his hand, and walked out of my mother's house and possibly out of her life for good. It was crazy because I went from having one parent walk out on me because of my sexuality to two parents. Whatever happened to parents are supposed to love their children in spite of? Whatever happened to the parent that told their children, 'I'll love you regardless'? Clearly, the love that my parents dished out had limits.

# CHAPTER 23

## Malaya Brown

*I* know, I know, I know! I said that I wouldn't set the bitch's studio on fire. But, having to do the walk of shame a few weeks ago at Texas Roadhouse because of Jarvis making a scene while damn near everybody was watched caused me to act irrationally. Yes, at first I was doing things because I was obsessed with Jarvis. Being in his presence and that one time he let me get a taste of his dick, it just had me acting out. Now, shit is different. Everything that I'm doing now and going forward is because I felt disrespected.

That day at the restaurant, Jarvis talked to me as if I was the scum of the earth, and I didn't like that. And when Malaya doesn't like something, she tends to act out and do reckless shit. I had a whole heap of shit that I planned to do, but I needed to get this tiny little thing out of the way first. Since Shonte worked in a plaza and I've pretty much studied the way that all of the cameras were placed, the plan that I had should run smoothly.

I had just parked my car about three blocks down, and I was dressed in all black with a skully on my head. The eyes and lips were cut out. I made my way up the stairs, careful to avoid being caught by the camera. Once I was in front of her door, I quickly kicked down the glass. I was already prepared for the alarm to go off, so my timing was perfect with everything that I had planned to do. Imagine the shock I got when after I shattered the glass, nothing happened. See, this was the reason why I couldn't stand this bitch now; she swore she couldn't be touched. This hoe was so damn confident that she didn't even put an alarm system on her studio, like shit was sweet.

After I had a hole in the glass, lord knows I wanted to run my ass in there, steal some of the merchandise, and possibly sell the shit on eBay. But it was a risk that I wasn't willing to take because I didn't know if anybody was going to come. I reached into the back pack that I had just taken off my back, and pulled out the gasoline that I had taken from under the kitchen counter at home.

I reached through the glass that I had kicked in, and I ended up hitting my arm on a piece of broken glass. That shit hurt so fuckin' bad that I wanted to scream out loud. I watched as the blood seeped out of my arms, and I had to quickly take the sweater off that I was wearing and wrap it over the cut. My blood on the floor would be a lot of evidence left behind. I was already prepared for something like this, so I poured the little bottle of bleach that I had in the backpack over the blood. I had been here long enough, so without further ado, I took the matches out, lit them, and threw them inside the studio. They landed right on top of all of the gasoline. I hurried up and got the fuck out of dodge because this bitch was about to start smoking in no time.

Once I made it to the other side of the street, I watched as her building that she had probably worked so hard for went up in flames. I jogged the three blocks to my car, and when I got inside, I was finally able to let off the scream that I wanted to because my fuckin' arm was in so much pain from scraping it with the glass. I removed the sweater from my hand and looked down at my arm. The cut was so disgusting that it turned my stomach. I couldn't go to the hospital with this, so I would just treat it when I got home.

Later that night when I made it home, I went to sleep with the biggest smile plastered on my face because of what I had accomplished tonight. I had something even bigger planned for tomorrow.

### The next day

For the past three hours, I had been in the parking lot where Javari attends school. I knew that sooner or later the teachers would bring the kids outside for recess. Now, while Shonte thought that she was doing something good by paying top dollar for her son to attend this school, she really wasn't doing a damn thing because these teachers who worked there were lazy as fuck, and ratchet as hell.

For about a week, I camped out in the parking lot area and watched as the teachers sat under the shade and didn't even pay attention to the kids as they were on the playground doing all types of dangerous shit. About five minutes later, Javari's teacher walked out with her students, which consisted of about fifteen kids in total. My eyes went right to Javari because he was the first one in the line. I'm not going to lie, that little boy was so handsome that I almost didn't want to do to him what I had in mind. I hated the bitch Shonte, but I will give credit where credit is due and say that she always had her son dressed nicely, and his long, pretty hair was always done.

Today, he was wearing a pair of tan Polo pants and a yellow and white Polo shirt. He had on a pair of wheat colored Timberland boots, and the little Cuban on his neck that I had seen him wearing on his birthday. I watched as the teacher said something to her students, and then a few seconds later, they all took off, heading toward the playground. That's when the teacher disappeared under the shade. I quickly made my way from my car over to the playground, with my scissors in hand.

When I made it, I had one hand behind my back, so that the scissors weren't obvious. I wasn't even standing there for a good two minutes before Javari spotted me and made his way over. Damn, I didn't even have to reel him in because he willingly came. Shonte and Jarvis should really teach their son about talking to strangers. Well, then again, I'm not a stranger because once upon a time, I had the potential to be his step mommy.

"You my mommy's friend," Javari said when he made his way over to me.

God, he was so fuckin' handsome. He was so innocent that I started to have doubts until I thought about the way his mother had left me for dead at the park, well in her case, thought she left me for dead, and then the way his father talked down to me at the restaurant. That was enough for me to say fuck second guessing what I was doing and go on with the plan.

"Well, can Mommy's friend have a hug?" I asked him.

He was hesitant at first, and then he walked over to me and wrapped his little arms around me. I used that moment to take my hand from behind me, which held the scissors, and I cut both of his long braids out of his head.

Javari must have felt the weight difference because he pushed me away from him and scowled at me, looking like the mini version of how his dad looked the other night when he was choking the shit out of me.

"Bitch! What the fuck did you do? My mama is going to beat your ass!" Javari cursed at me.

I took off running, and his little bad ass ran behind me, but his little legs couldn't keep up with a grown woman. When I made it to my car, I threw his hair in the passenger seat and got the fuck out of dodge. All the cursing that Javari was doing had caused his teacher to come out of hiding to see what the fuck was going on.

When I made it to the light, I was dying laughing at the shit that I had just done. I picked up his hair, examined it and cursed myself because had I cut just a little bit more of it, I could have turned this into some bundles because that little boy had some good ass hair. He was right about one thing; his mother was going to beat my ass. The thing was, I was a hard bitch to find, so I doubt that she would find me anytime soon. I had caused enough damage in only two days, so after this, I was going into hiding. I no longer had the phone that I normally had because I had high reasons to believe that Jarvis would somehow track me down. Lord knows that I didn't need him finding me.

Right now, I was using a little flip phone, but it got the job done.

I really didn't have anybody to call because I had pretty much killed everybody, except for my dad. Speaking of my dad, I needed to call and check up on him because I hadn't talked to him in weeks. I loved my dad because after I came out of the institution, he took me in, and not once did he judge me or look at me with those accusing eyes like my bitch ass sister and my mother did.

In fact, he had never once asked me about Tank, and I loved him for that. In the years that I spent in Virginia with him, we had established a bond that could never be broken, and because of that, I will always love him. I've just been so preoccupied lately, that I didn't have time to call him.

When I made it home, I noticed that the police car was parked in my driveway. I sucked my teeth because I knew that it was nobody but those detectives coming back to fuck with me. I threw the hair that I had in the passenger seat into the glove compartment as I pulled up in the driveway. When I got out, I noticed that it was only Detective Davis who got out of the car. I would have rather it have been Detective Tony. Detective Davis wasn't falling for the bullshit that was coming out of my mouth, but I think I had Detective Tony fooled.

"You're a hard girl to track down, Ms. Malaya Brown," Davis told me once I had made it close enough.

The evil in me wanted to reach in my purse, pull out my scissors, and stab his ass to death. But I'd be a fool to think that I could get away with murdering a cop.

"That's because I didn't know that I had someone tracking me down, so why should I stay home, waiting for them to find me?" I asked, reaching up to pull a strand of hair out of my face.

When I did, I watched as his eyes fell to the big Band-Aid that I had on my arm, which still had dried up blood in it. I needed stiches because my skin was literally split apart and the bone in my arm was visible, but I wasn't fuckin' with the hospital like that. When I got home last night, I poured some Peroxide on it and just placed a big ass Band-Aid on top.

"What happened to your arm?" he asked, just like I knew he would.

"Nothing that I can't handle. Why are you over here, and where is Tony? Isn't he your partner? Shouldn't y'all travel together at all times," I asked him, crossing my arms and cocking my head to the side for emphasis.

"Malaya Brown. Remember I kept saying that name sounded familiar. This house even looked familiar, but I just couldn't put my fuckin' finger on the shit. Years ago, when I started out as a cop, I got a call to come down to this house because it was your mother reported to me that she witnessed you stabbing your ex-boyfriend in your room," he told me.

I looked at him strangely because I know for a fact that I was home alone that day. My mom was at work and wouldn't have been home any time soon.

"Judging by your facial expression, I'm pretty sure you know just what the hell I'm referring to? I remember you, Malaya, I also remember the day I came in here, placed those handcuffs on you, and put you in the backseat of my car. So, what happened? Years later, you found out that it was your mother who had placed the anonymous call to us about her daughter stabbing her ex-boyfriend to death, and that's the reason why all of a sudden you mother just disappeared?" Detective Davis asked me.

Even though it sounded that way, it wasn't the case at all. Yes, I killed my mother, but it wasn't for that. Damn, so no wonder she always looked at me the way that she did. She was the one to catch me in the act and call the damn police on my ass. Where the fuck was the loyalty? I definitely didn't regret offing her ass now!

"If you think that I would kill my mother over some shit that happened years ago, then clearly you got me fucked up!" I told him, walking away.

"But you would kill her for something else right? Is that what you're saying?" he probed, coming closer to me. Davis was going to be a fuckin' problem, and the sad part about it, there wasn't shit that I could do to make his ass go away.

"Stop trying to put fuckin' words in my mouth, man. Is this what the fuck you came over here for? To get me to confess to some bullshit story that you just made up in your head?" I asked him. There was a long pause and then I looked up at him and let off a chuckle. "Damn, you really let yourself go, Davis. I remember when you put me in the back of your car. I was only fifteen years old, but the way your sexy ass looked in that police uniform had my pussy dripping wet back then. Look at you now! Lay off on the coffee and donuts," I told him. Finally getting the chance to take in his appearance, I knew then that he was the same cop who had come to arrest me years ago.

"Let's see who the fuck gets the last laugh when I come back in here with enough evidence to take your ass away to prison for good. It won't be any shit about you pleading insanity this time. I'm going to make sure that your ass gets charged with murder for Mya Brown, Malaya Brown, Teresa Brown, and last, but not least, Deon Hilton," he said, shocking the hell out of me when he mentioned Deon's name. "I'm coming for your ass, Malaya, so enjoy your freedom while you can," he told me and then walked back to his car.

# CHAPTER 24

## Shonte Banks

Today was just like any other day. I woke up, got myself and my son ready for school, and by 8:30, I was in the car dropping Javari to school. I pulled up to the plaza where my studio was and there were a bunch of police cars in the parking lot, along with yellow police tape to stop anybody from going up the stairs. Immediately, my heart began to beat rapidly as I jumped out of the car and made my way over to where all of the police officers were standing.

"Ma'am, you can't be over here," one of the cops said, grabbing my arm and pushing me out of the way.

I silently thanked God that Jarvis was not with me. Jarvis wouldn't give two fucks about a badge, he would have beat this cop's ass for man handling me the way that he just did. There was too much shit going on now with cops, so I decided to keep it cool and not let what he just did piss me off, even though I was steaming mad.

"That's my studio up there. What the fuck is going on?" I asked him.

"Which studio is yours?" he asked me.

"The one right there. Lovely Faces," I told him.

I tried to go around him, so that I could point to it, but the only thing that was left was the letter S from the word faces. My body became numb, and I didn't know what the fuck to do. Something that I had worked so hard for, and my father had invested so much money into this property, and a jealous, vindictive bitch does some shit like this! It didn't take a rocket scientist to know that Malaya was the one to cause this damage.

"My team is on it, ma'am. They are watching the cameras now to see who did this," the policeman let me know.

I had no words for him, so I walked away and pulled my phone out of my purse so that I could call my husband. I was sick and tired of holding in the way that I felt, so Jarvis was about to get a piece of my fuckin' mind right now!

"What's good, baby? I was just about to call your ass. Fuck I tell you about leaving the house without waking me up?" Jarvis snapped into the phone.

Most days, Jarvis didn't have to be to the center until about eleven, so he slept later than I did, which is why I didn't want to wake him. Clearly, that wasn't important at the moment.

"Jarvis, that's really the least of my fuckin' concerns right now! I'm fuckin pissed at you right now because you allowed this shit! First, I lose my baby, this bitch comes to my son birthday party with her little gift, then the hoe had the fuckin balls to pop her ass up at my parents' house while we were on vacation. I come to work this morning and this hoe has burned my studio down to the fuckin' ground, Jarvis!" I screamed at him as I sat in the car with tears flowing down my face. I was crying tears of frustration right now. I just wanted to reach out and touch this bitch so that she could feel me!

"First off, don't you ever in your muthafuckin' life blame me for some fucked up shit that another bitch done caused! By you doing that, you pretty much saying that I support it. If that's the case, do you really think I'm down for another bitch causing you to lose our baby, Shonte? Tighten the fuck up and come at me correct the next time! I'm sorry that shit happened to your studio, baby, I really am, but come on, that shit can be replaced, you can't! Imagine if she did some fucked up shit like that while you were in there or something? I would lose my fuckin' mind if something happened to you!" Jarvis told me.

I couldn't even say anything to what he had just said, so let the angry tears continue to fall from my face.

"Don't tell the police shit either. I want to handle this bitch personally. Go on over to my sister's house, and I'll meet you over there," Jarvis told me.

I didn't even bother to respond, I just hung up the phone on him. I knew I was wrong for saying that shit out of my mouth to him, it's just that I was mad and I was looking for someone to point the finger at. I felt so bad for saying it because it was kind of coming off like I blamed him for causing me to lose the baby, and Lord knows that I never blamed Jarvis for that at all.

About an hour later, I pulled up to La'shay's house. The reason I took so long to get there is because I kept driving in circles, making sure that bitch wasn't following me. Once I knew that I was straight, I pulled into a parking space at the apartment complex where La'shay stayed. I got out of my car with a heavy heart. I bragged and took pride in having my own business, and just that quick, it was taken away from me. I dreaded having to call my daddy and let him know that had happened because I know that he would be just as pissed, if not more than I was.

I walked up to La'shay's door and waited for her to answer. Today was Monday, and lucky for me, La'shay is off on Mondays. A minute later, she came to the door and opened it for me. She stood before me in some Nike workout clothes, and she had a bonnet on her head. When I walked into her home, I noticed that she had a whole bunch of moving boxes in her living room area. I also noticed that the majority of the artwork that she used to have hanging up on the walls was now gone. I looked at this bitch and just shook my head.

"When the hell were you going to tell me you were moving?" I asked her as I flopped down on her couch and threw my head back. A bitch was stressing for real, and Lord knows I needed a drink, but that was clearly out of the question.

"Later on today because I needed you to help me clean out the closet," she told me with a laugh, and then plopped down right next to me.

As I rested my head on the back of the couch, I had my eyes closed, and that feeling of wanting to cry again came over me.

"Oh Lord, what my brother done did now?" Shay asked me.

I chucked a little bit because every time she saw me upset, she always assumed that it was because of some shit that her brother had done.

"Not him this time. It was that bitch Malaya. The lil hoe burned down my studio," I said.

It's like when I said it, it sounded so real and because of that, I got pissed off all over again.

"That bitch did what?" La'shay asked, jumping up off the couch and throwing the bonnet off of her head. "Shonte, that bitch doing all of this because clearly she doesn't think you or my brother is a threat. Fuck, you should have killed that hoe when you had the chance!" La'shay said, referring to the story that I had told her about Malaya and I getting into the fight at the park. When I choked the shit out of her and thought that I had killed her.

La'shay told me that to make sure that she was dead, I should have used my gun and shot her, but for some reason, I was so scared to catch my first body. All I kept thinking about was my son. Like what if something went wrong and I got caught and had to spend the rest of my life behind bars? I would never get to see the light of day again and the feeling of not waking up and seeing my son every day killed me. Shit has changed since then, though. I knew that if I went into this thing prepared, that I could take Malaya out because I was sick and tired of this bitch thinking that she couldn't be touched.

La'shay and I continued to talk about the whole Malaya situation, until my phone started ringing. I panicked because I noticed that it was my son's school and I had a feeling that this couldn't be good.

I stood up from the couch and answered the phone. "Hello?" I answered.

"Hello, this is Principal Jenkins calling from Greater Kid's Academy, is this Javari's mother?" the principal asked me.

"Yes, is everything alright with my son?" I asked her, silently praying that I wasn't about to hear some more bullshit today.

"Well, Javari had an incident today during recess, which is why I'm calling you. From what Javari told us, one of your friends came onto the playground area where he was and she cut off your son's hair and—"

"How the fuck did a bitch even get so close to my son, that she was able to cut his hair without his teacher being there to stop it?" I barked into the phone, cutting her off from whatever the fuck was about to come out of her mouth. At the end of the day, this was the principal that I was talking to, so she should always have her children in check. Because of that, she was going to be the one to feel my wrath.

"Mrs. Banks, please calm down. Trust me, the teacher has already been disciplined and—"

"Disciplined? I want that bitch fired. What the fuck was she doing that was so important that she wasn't able to have control of her class? You know what? I'll be there in about ten minutes. If disciplined meant that you sent that that bitch home, then good for you because if not, you better plan accordingly because I'm slapping the fuck out of her when I get there!" I said, ending the call.

I didn't even have to tell La'shay what happened because she was right on my heels as I walked out the door.

Just like I said, in ten minutes, I was walking into the building.

Because I was already pissed off, it was no telling the shit I might do once I made it to the principal's office. All of the police officers that worked there, which was about four of them were there when I walked in. *Did this bitch really call the cops for me?* Then again, I did make a threat over the phone, so I guess she had to do what she had to do.

I wasn't even in the building a good minute before my son ran over to me with half of his hair gone. The bitch had cut the long braids that fell down to his back. Seeing him like that was enough to make me act real ignorant.

"This what the fuck am I'm paying top dollar for every month? The amount of money I give y'all a fuckin' year is almost equivalent to somebody's college tuition! Then y'all have the nerve to bring the damn cops in here because of some shit that I said over the phone! Shouldn't these muthafuckas be somewhere watching a camera to see who cut off my baby's hair?" I barked at everybody who was in the damn office.

These white people were looking at me in shock with the shit that was flying out of my mouth. I tried to never use profanity in front of my son, but I was way too hot right now not to.

"Shonte, chill. These crackers, gon' fuck around and take your ass to jail," La'shay whispered, trying to get me to calm down.

"So that's it? A bitch don't get no apology or nothing? I'm just supposed to be okay with the fact that my son was dropped off early this morning with a head full of hair and now he isn't! Y'all looking at me like I'm fuckin' crazy for wanting to know how is it that something like this happened while my son was under y'all watch!" I seethed.

"Mrs. Banks, we assure you that his teacher has been fired, if that's what you wanted to know," Principal Jenkins finally brought her scary ass from the back and said.

She was an older lady, maybe in her late fifties, but she could pass for thirty. I used to have the utmost respect for her because at orientation, she said all of the right things, which is why I decided to bring my son to this expensive ass school in the first place. I was looking at her a little bit differently now. All I saw was a lady who didn't give a fuck about these children, she just cared about making sure we paid that damn money every month. I just didn't see any compassion or sympathy in her eyes for what happened to my son.

"You know what? Fuck it! This will be the last time y'all ever see my son because best believe today was his last day here!" I said, turning around to pick my son up.

We walked out of the building together. How the fuck was I supposed to explain this shit to his daddy without him going to fuckin' jail? When we made it to the car, I called Kiondre to see if he could do Javari's hair. There was no sense in me having my baby walk around here with some trick daddy braids, so I was just going to have Kiondre cut it into a short cut.

"Who cut your hair, Javari?" I asked, looking at him through the rearview mirror.

"Your friend," he told me, and I already knew who he was referring to. "I called her a bitch, and told her that you were going to beat her ass," my son added.

La'shay burst out laughing, spitting out the water she was drinking. I just shook my head. Any other time, I would have popped the shit out of Javari for cursing, but I can honestly say right now, that I understood why he did it. He's a fuckin' little boy, and for a grown woman to do some shit like that to him, that shit was crazy. Plus, Javari had inherited my attitude.

"Don't talk like that, Javari! I am going to beat her ass though," I said, getting a little laugh out of him.

"I'm not even mad about having to cut my hair, Ma. I'm tired of people thinking that I'm a little girl. The other day in school, one of the teachers kept saying that I was so pretty. I had to tell her to call me handsome because all of the girls call me handsome," Javari said.

I looked at him and shook my head. Clearly, I was about to have a little Jarvis on my hands.

Later on that day, when we made it home, I noticed that Jarvis's car was in the driveway. God, I wasn't prepared for him to see Javari's hair like this, but I sucked it up and got out of the car. I'm not going to lie, Javari looked so handsome with his little cut, that I kept taking pictures of him. When we made it into the house, I took my shoes off by the front door and went in search of my husband.

"Baby?" I called out once I saw that he wasn't in the den.

"I'm in the room," he called back to me.

I took the stairs two at a time until I made it up to the room. When I got inside, I noticed that Jarvis was back and forth from the closet to the bedroom, placing clothes in a suitcase. I looked at him oddly because he didn't mention anything to me about going out of town.

"Where you going?" I asked, looking in the suitcase to see what he had packed.

"Out of town, and before I leave, I'm putting you and Javari in a hotel," he told me.

It was almost as if what he said was final and he wasn't expecting me to say anything else about it, but I've never been the one to not have an opinion on something, especially something that I didn't like.

"Where are you going, Jarvis? And why do we have to stay in a hotel?" I asked, folding my arms across my chest.

"Because, Shonte, this bitch is testing my gangsta, and what type of man would I be if I let this bitch continue to wreak havoc? I'm about to handle some shit out in Virginia, and I'll be able to concentrate more, knowing that my wife, my son, and my unborn child are somewhere tucked away where the bitch can't find you!" Jarvis told me.

"What the fuck is in Virginia?" I asked him, confused as hell.

"Her daddy," Jarvis told me with a devilish look on his handsome face.

"Well, I'm going too!" I said, jumping off the bed and going into the closet to get my Louis Vuitton luggage.

"Shonte, now ain't the fuckin' time for you to try and go against what I'm doing! If you're going to pack a bag, pack one for you and my son so that I can put y'all up in a hotel down here until I leave!" he barked at me, grabbing my arm.

"No!" I said, stomping my feet like a spoiled ass child, who didn't get their way. "You promised me, Jarvis! You promised that when you got at the bitch, that you would let me in! You promised!" I cried to him.

I couldn't let him take this moment away from me. She was the one who had caused me the most pain, so whatever Jarvis had in mind, I wanted in.

"Fuck, man!" Jarvis grunted, as he went and took a seat at the edge of the bed. I knew then that I had my way.

A few seconds later, Javari came into the room. "Look at my haircut, Dad," he told Jarvis, going over to show his daddy his new haircut.

Jarvis looked at me with murder in his eyes, and before he could say something, I quickly said spoke up.

"It wasn't me! Malaya came down to the school and cut his braids, so I took him to Kiondre so he could cut the rest off," I said, all in one breath.

Jarvis and I had an agreement that whenever we made big moves, we would talk to each other about it first. Javari's hair was a big move, so I could see why Jarvis was looking at me with murderous eyes.

"Hurry up and pack a bag before I go back to fuckin' prison," Jarvis said, pulling his suitcase off the bed and walking out of the room with our son. I literally just threw anything into the suitcase, and in about five more minutes, we were walking out of the door. The first stop was to drop Javari off to La'shay's house, since Malaya didn't know where she lived.

"I got all types of guns in the back, so I hope you know we driving, and this is about a fourteen-hour drive," Jarvis told me and I nodded my head.

Since we were going out of town, I called down to the doctor's office and cancelled my appointment for in the morning. It's crazy because I was actually looking forward to that appointment tomorrow because I would find out the sex of the baby.

# CHAPTER 25

## Jarvis Banks

The perks of being in the streets back then came in handy today because it allowed me to get inside information on people. I had a white buddy named Greg, and his ass was a fuckin genius when it came to computer hacking and shit like that. I never really felt the need to hit his ass up because there was no reason to. Number one, I'm an eye for an eye type of nigga. You do something to me or my family, I'm doing something back, but the only difference is that I'm coming back ten times harder.

Malaya killed my son, whom I never even got the pleasure of meeting. Since she didn't have a son, I would kill the next thing closest to her, which was her sister, but it was too late because the bitch was already dead. So, I figured that I may as well get at that bitch's mama, but imagine my surprise when I saw a missing person's picture of her mother the other day while I was out. Her mother wasn't missing though, Malaya had offed her ass, and that was obvious as hell. So, a nigga was defeated because I had no one else to resort to, until I hit up my homie Greg and he was able to tell me about Malaya's daddy that she had tucked away in Virginia.

That information was enough to make my dick hard because I needed somebody close to this bitch. I wanted her to know what it felt like to have somebody take something away from you that you loved dearly. Even though I never got the chance to meet Justin or my unborn, I loved them dearly, and they were both taken away from me by the hands of that bitch.

That night when I choked Malaya out at Texas Roadhouse, I could have easily killed her, but visons of my mother, my sister, my wife, and my son kept popping up in my head, and I knew that it was no way possible that I was going to let a bitch like Malaya cause me to leave my family again. This time, it would be forever because if I murdered her in a room filled with people, there would be no coming out.

As far as bringing Shonte with me, that was the last thing I wanted to do, but like she said, I did promise her that whatever I had planned, I would let her in on, I would even let her be the one to pull the trigger. I had never been the type of nigga to want to be on some Bonnie & Clyde type of shit. If you ask me, only dumb niggas would like that shit because what real nigga in their right mind would be content with bussing guns next to their bitch? Let alone, let another nigga bust his guns at her. Fuck no! I would rather do the dirty work and then come home to my girl, but it's like I can see it in Shonte's eyes that killing Malaya is some shit that she won't rest until she gets the opportunity to do.

We had been in Virginia for two days, and every day, I would park my car on the other side and just watch the house where Malaya's father lived. It reminded me of somewhere on a damn farm. All of the houses were pretty much spread apart, and the backyards were big as hell.

I picked up on this nigga's habits in only two days, and from the looks of things, he was the only one staying there. He would leave out every morning around nine, and wouldn't come home until about five that evening. I don't know where he worked, but each time he left, he would be dressed casually in some slacks and a polo. I had already made up in my mind though that tonight was the night that I would make my move.

"Follow my lead. Don't make any moves without me telling your ass to!" I told Shonte, who was sitting casually in the passenger seat.

"Okay, Jarvis! You don't have to keep telling me this!" she snapped at me.

I looked at her for a few more seconds, and then I got out of the car with her following me. It was dark as hell out there because this country ass neighborhood didn't have any damn street lights.

"Stay behind me," I told Shonte once we made it in front of the door.

She went got behind me and then I knocked, covering the peephole with my hand.

"Who is it?" her father asked from the other side of the door.

I ignored him as I held my hand over the hole, and my other hand on my gun. As soon as I heard him turn the doorknob, I rushed his ass, knocking him upside the head with the butt of my gun. He immediately fell over, holding onto his head, which had blood seeping out of it. I quickly went and pushed the door closed behind me, making sure to lock it.

"Listen here, old man, we can do this the easy way or we can do this the hard way. Doesn't really matter because both will result in you dying in the end. Get your phone out and call your daughter," I told him as I squatted before him.

"Whatt... what... are you talking about?" he cried, still holding onto his face.

"Your fuckin' daughter, nigga! Malaya fuckin' Brown. Don't play stupid or I'll blow your fuckin' brains out right here," I barked at him.

"I don't have her number. She changed it, I swear, man!" he cried.

For some reason, I didn't believe him.

"Let me see your phone, man. If I find out you lying, I'm killing your ass," I told him.

He slowly got up and made his way to where his phone was as I followed him with the gun trained on the back of his head, just in case his old ass tried something stupid. He showed me his phone, which was on the kitchen table and I flipped it open. I went through his contacts, found where he had Malaya's contact and I called it. Lucky for him, he was telling the truth about her changing her number. I went through his call log and noticed that two days ago, he had a missed call from a Miami area code. Suspicion got the best of me, so I called the number. I waited a few for the caller to pick up, and then her voice came through the line.

"Heyy, Daddy! I called you the other day," she cooed into the phone.

One would never think that a voice so innocent could be so fuckin' evil. I quickly hung the phone up because nothing was planned yet, and we couldn't go into this thing unprepared. Even though Malaya was labeled insane, the bitch wasn't fuckin' stupid.

"She's going to call you back, and when she does, I want you to sound happier than a muthafucka! Tell her that you won the fuckin mega millions and that she needs to come out here so you can give her some money," I told him.

There was no sense in me coming on the phone and letting her know that if I could kill her daddy right now because most likely, this evil bitch would give me the okay to go ahead and off his ass. The thing about money though, it will make people do some crazy shit, so I know if she heard about her daddy winning all of that money, she would be on the next thing smoking.

"Wipe your face, old man. Get a little happy," I told him, laughing while the gun was still pressed against his head. Once he pulled himself together, it was like clockwork that Malaya started calling him back.

"Heyy, Princess," he answered.

"What happened, Daddy? Why did you hang up the phone?" she asked him.

"I'm sorry, Princess, you know how this flip phone is, but I was calling to let you know some good news. That mega millions that I'm always playing, I finally won all of that money. I was calling to see if you wanted to come down here with me and we can go and pick up the money tomorrow," her dad said.

"What? Daddy, are you serious?" she asked him.

I could hear the excitement in her voice.

"I'm serious, Malaya. You're my only child, and the only person that I have to split all of this money with. What is my old ass going to do with millions of dollars?" he asked, getting her to laugh.

"Tell her to take a plane," I mouthed to him.

"Baby girl, just go ahead and look up some plane tickets. I'll give you the money for it."

"Oh no, Daddy, that's fine, I will drive. I will be there sometime tomorrow. I love you," she said, and then she hung up the phone.

"Why did I tell you we were going to drive?" I asked, focusing my attention on Shonte.

"Because of the guns," she told me. She thought about it for a minute and then shook her head. "This bitch is planning to kill her daddy so that she can have all of that money," Shonte said and then shook her head.

This was what I mean when I said money will make people do some crazy shit.

We walked into the den area, pointed to the La-Z-Boy and told his ass where to sit. "Go in the car and bring me that rope that's in the backseat," I told Shonte, handing her my keys.

I didn't want to risk leaving this man alone because I didn't know if he had guns stashed somewhere in this house. When Shonte left, he turned his head and looked at me, with pleading eyes.

"Why you doing this to me, man? What did my daughter do that was so bad that I have to pay for it?" he cried.

I would have felt bad for him, but the images of my wife laying up in the hospital bed after she miscarried just wouldn't allow me to.

"You saw that beautiful woman that just walked out of here?" I asked him. He weakly shook his head yes. "Your daughter, or your princess, since that what you like to call her, she killed our fuckin' baby! Set my wife's studio on fire and then the bitch chopped off my son's hair. Not to mention, she murdered my other son. A son I never even got the chance to meet. That's why I'm going to kill your daughter. Well, my wife is going to kill your daughter."

I laughed, and the same time, Shonte walked in and handed the rope to me. I tied up his hands and his feet because I wasn't trying to take any chances.

"Go look in there and see if this nigga got something to eat! I'm hungry as fuck," I told Shonte.

She came back a few minutes later with a box of Ritz crackers and a water. She handed them to me and then took a seat next to me on the couch.

"Why I feel like you only brought me here so that you could order me around?" she asked, causing me to chuckle lightly.

"You damn right!" I told her then reached over and kissed her forehead.

Shonte rested her head on my chest, and a few minutes later, I heard light snores coming from her. I was too much in a rage to go to sleep, so I sat there and waited the fourteen hours that it would take for Malaya to get there.

***Midnight the next day***

Finally, I heard a knock at the door.

"Stay right here," I told Shonte and then got up from the couch.

I made my way to the door and quickly opened it. When Malaya saw me standing there, she immediately tried to take off and run, but I grabbed her hair and I got the surprise of my life. The wig that she had on slipped right through my fingers, causing it to fall off and me to stare at her bald head. A head that was damn near balder than mine. I ran up to her and grabbed her into me by the back of the hoodie she was wearing.

"Why you running from me now, baby girl?" I asked, pulling her into the house with me.

"What the fuck did you do to my daddy?" she screamed once the door was closed.

"I didn't do nothing to him yet, but hold on right quick!" I said, taking the gun from the back of my pants pocket. I let off two rounds into her father's skull. "One for each child of mine that you killed," I told her as I ended her father's life.

"Daddy!" she screamed, walking over to him and holding onto his dead body.

"Bitch please, cut the bullshit because you know just like I know that you brought your ass over here today to murder this man! Isn't that why you chose to drive instead of getting on a plane?' I asked, walking over to her.

She looked up at me and let out a laugh. "Alright, alright, you got me! But it's your bitch who I want!" she said.

It happened so fast. She reached in the waist of her jeans and focused the gun on Shonte.

"Shonte, move!" I screamed at her.

Shonte moved just in time before Malaya let her gun off. That gun was small, but it was powerful as hell. I didn't even feel that shit when I had jacked her ass up. Malaya was so worried about trying to aim for Shonte, that she never even saw me coming. I shot her one good time in the hand that she used to pull the trigger, and she dropped the gun. Shonte quickly walked up on me, took the gun out of my hand, and let off two shots into Malaya. She wasn't aiming at spots that could instantly kill her. She was going for her ankles, hands and shit.

"I don't want to kill her! Let's bury her alive!" Shonte said. I looked at her like she was crazy. Clearly, her ass had been watching too many damn movies. "Seriously, Jarvis! I saw the shovel in the backyard!"

I looked at all of that land in the back yard and the idea didn't sound so bad at all. The same rope that I once had on Malaya's father, I used to tie her up with.

"Jarvis, remember when you let me give you head at GG's? Damn, that dick tasted so good," Malaya said, instantly pissing Shonte off.

She walked over to her and slapped the shit out of her with the butt of the gun. "I knew about that already, hoe! But did you fuck him though? No, I don't think so!" Shonte answered her own question. "Ewww, what the fuck?" she screamed.

I looked down to see what the fuck was going on, and Malaya's dentures were on the fuckin' floor.

"I knew them teeth were too straight. I'm disgusted with myself! Fuckin' with a bitch with no fuckin' teeth or hair," I said.

I grabbed some tape and placed it over Malaya's mouth because she kept saying shit to piss off my wife. We went outside to the backyard and I came up out of my shirt and went to digging. I ain't never done no shit like this, but leave it to Shonte to have me digging a hole six feet deep. Damn near three hours later, I had we hole deep enough.

"Go ahead and bring her, baby," I told Shonte.

She gladly got up from the patio chair she was sitting in and kicked Malaya's body over to me, all the while, she was humming and moaning with that tape on her mouth. It was too late for her to beg for her life now. Once Shonte had her to the edge, she kicked her body inside, and Malaya took a long fall. She landed on her back. I blew her a kiss and then threw all of the dirt that I had just dug up back on top of her.

"I give it about eight minutes before she dies in there," I told Shonte.

"What about her daddy?" Shonte asked me, pointing toward the house.

"Well, Malaya likes fire, so it's only right that we send his ass out in style," I said, releasing a sinister laugh.

We walked back into the house. I kept in my back pocket, since I liked to spark up a blunt anywhere I'm at, so I took it out and walked over to her father's dead body. I put the lighter to the shirt that he was wearing, and just that quick, the fire began to spread.

"Let's go," I told Shonte, and we walked out the door hand in hand.

I don't know what the hell it was, maybe it was God, but that same song that Shonte used to sing to me years ago started playing on the radio. I smiled as she sang the words to me.

"I've got a real thing, here by my side. Someone who needs me, holding me tight. And these special feelings, won't ever fade, 'cause I knew from the start, you put a move on my heart," Shonte sang to me as we watched the house go up into flames and I drove away.

"You really love a nigga, huh?" I asked her.

"I loved you since I was fifteen, Jarvis. I just love you more now because I really know what love is," she told me and reached over to kiss my cheek.

"I love your ass more. What I just did proved that I will not allow a nigga or a bitch to fuck with you or my kids. Also, just know that you changed me, man, but for the better. Just like how you say I put a move on your heart, you put one on mine too."

# EPILOGUE

# Ashanti Palmer

*One year Later*

For the past year, I have been working on loving me for the first time in probably forever. I learned that I couldn't expect God to please me if I wasn't doing the right things to receive a blessing. With Chad, I almost feel like I forced him to love me. I wanted to get the sweetest revenge on my ex best friend, and I ended up lying down with her man and then having a baby by him. I guess that saying is true about the same way you get him is the same way that you lose him because I lost Chad, and to a man at that.

Right now, my main priority was to raise my daughter, Ariel and continue to save this money. In another month or so, I will finally have enough money for the deposit on my own shop. Lord knows I didn't plan on working for Kiondre for the rest of my life. As far as Shonte and I go, I wish her the best, even though I know that she will never in her life be friends with me again, and I can't fault her for that.

That's enough about me, though; I'm just taking it one day at a time. This time, when it comes to a relationship, I'm not going to look for love. I'm going to let love find me, and when it does, I'm going to make sure it's with a single man, not someone who I have to sneak around with and force him to love me. Lord knows I can't have another bitch beat my ass the way Shonte did.

# Chad Williams

After my mom and I got into that heated argument, I came at her one more time to see if she had changed her mind, but sadly, she hadn't. If she couldn't accept me for who I am, then that's fine. I'm not going to lie; I miss my mother every day, but she caused this. I didn't see how my desire for men would be enough for her to wash her hands of me, but it was. Tony and I were still going strong, and we even moved into our own house together. For the first time, in a long ass time, I was fuckin' happy because I was finally being true to myself.

Luckily, I didn't have the baby mama from hell because Ashanti didn't use me being gay against me. She allowed me to have my daughter on the weekends, and I was fine with that. Now, I don't know what Ashanti may say about me behind closed doors, but I just love her for not judging me in front of my face. Who would have ever thought that the one I brought the most headache and pain to would be the one telling me, "Fuck anybody who has a problem with me being gay." I wished my mom would have the same compassion as Ashanti did.

# Shonte Banks

"*I* see your ass trying to peek and shit. Shonte, chill before you fuck up the surprise," Jarvis told me, reaching over and squeezing my thigh.

I was riding shotgun in his car. I had our son in the back, our baby girl Shaniya in the car seat, and a bun in the oven. I guess you can say that I'm one of those females that you just look at and I pop up pregnant, because here I was pregnant again. I'll admit, my pregnancy with my daughter had a lot of complications, mainly because I was stressed a lot, and the image of Malaya and her father haunted me at night, causing me to have Shaniya at eight months. Now, a whole year later, Malaya was a thing of the past. Jarvis and I didn't even bring her up.

Anyway, right now, I sat in the car, anticipating this surprise that Mr. Banks had in store for me. Finally, I felt the car come to a stop.

"Stay right there. Javari, let me know if she peeking and shit," Jarvis told our son, causing him to laugh.

"I got you, Daddy," Javari said from behind me.

A few seconds later, I felt the door being opened. Jarvis helped me out, and then I felt a tiny hand hold mine, so I assume Javari came around to hold my hand for me. At the same time, I could hear my baby girl making gurgling noises, so she must have been out of the car as well. I didn't know where we were going, but eventually we stopped and Jarvis removed the scarf from over my eyes. When I opened them, we were standing in front of a building, which was called Lovely Faces. Out front stood my mom, my dad, La'shay, Tez, and all of Jarvis' family.

"Every time that bitch fucked something up, it was like you won because I came around and gave you bigger and better, baby. This all you!" Jarvis said, placing two keys in my hand.

"Thank you, baby, so much. God, I fuckin' love you," I said, pulling him into me and raining kisses all over his face.

My baby was the truth for real. For years, I had yearned for the day that Jarvis would grow the fuck up and be the faithful man that I wanted him to be, and it finally happened. It may not have been when I wanted it to, but it damn sure happened. I tried to convince myself that I loved Chad while Javris was away, but Jarvis came right back in and put a move on my heart. I knew that there was nobody else alive who I would want to spend forever with.

## THE END

*Stay on the lookout for La'shay and Devontez' story; Lovin' a Hustler*

Join our mailing list to get a notification when Leo Sullivan Presents has another release!
Text **LEOSULLIVAN** to **22828** to join!

To submit a manuscript for our review, email us at <u>leosullivanpresents@gmail.com</u>

# Get LiT!

*Download the LiT eReader app today and enjoy exclusive content, free books, and more*

CPSIA information can be obtained
at www.ICGtesting.com
Printed in the USA
LVOW10s1949080518
576442LV00010B/1056/P